The Materializing of Duncan McTavish

Also available in the Road to Avonlea Series

The Journey Begins
The Story Girl Earns Her Name
Song of the Night
Quarantine at Alexander Abraham's
Conversions

Next in the Series

Aunt Abigail's Beau
Malcolm and the Baby
Felicity's Challenge

The Materializing of Duncan McTavish

Storybook written by
Heather Conkie

Based on the Sullivan Films Production
adapted from the novels of

Lucy Maud Montgomery

HarperCollins*Publishers*Ltd

THE MATERIALIZING OF DUNCAN MCTAVISH
Storybook written by Heather Conkie

Copyright © 1991 by HarperCollins Publishers Ltd,
Sullivan Films, Inc., Ruth Macdonald and David Macdonald

Based on the Sullivan Films Production produced by Sullivan Films Inc.
in association with CBC and the Disney Channel with the participation of
Telefilm Canada adapted from Lucy Maud Montgomery's novels.

Teleplay written by Heather Conkie
Copyright © 1989 by Heather Conkie

Canadian Cataloguing in Publication Data
Conkie, Heather
The materializing of Duncan McTavish
(Road to Avonlea; #4)
Based on the t.v. series: Road to Avonlea.
ISBN 0-00-647036-X
I. Title. II. Series.
PS8555.054M3 1991   jC813'.54   C91-093297-2
PZ7.C65Ma 1991

Design by Andrew Smith Graphics Inc.
91 92 93 94 95 OFF 10 9 8 7 6 5 4 3 2 1

Chapter One

Outside the village of Avonlea, past the covered bridge and along the road that curves beside the King farm and its orchards, stands a storybook cottage, complete with freshly painted white gingerbread trim and a neat picket fence. At this time of year, the lattices on the shady front porch are resplendent with climbing roses of all colors and varieties, hence the name, Rose Cottage.

As the rays of the morning sun sought out the shadowy corners of the porch and touched the dewy petals of the roses with warmth, the front door suddenly opened and Hetty King appeared. She was a tall, thin woman dressed severely in a dark skirt and high-necked, spotless white blouse, its only decoration a small watch pinned to its crisp bodice. There was not a hair on her head out of place as she energetically shook out a lace table-cloth. Her voice carried through the stillness of the morning.

"Sara should be up by now, don't you think, Olivia? I'm sure people sleep till noon in Montreal, but such lackadaisical ways won't do in this house!" She took a deep, therapeutic breath of fresh morning air and disappeared back into the house.

A light knocking on her bedroom door dragged an unwilling Sara Stanley from the comfortable depths of sleep. She pulled her eider-down over her rumpled blond head, tucked it closer around her ears and wished fervently to return to the fascinating dream she had been in the middle of dreaming.

The knocking persisted, however, and her Aunt Olivia's voice floated through the air.

"Sara, dear! It's time you were awake. We have a million things to do before the sewing circle meets today."

Sara groaned inwardly. It all came flooding back to her now. Today was the day she would have to endure her first Avonlea sewing circle.

For the first time since arriving in the village

some months ago, Sara had begun to feel truly at home. At first, she was sure that the pain of not being with her beloved father in Montreal would be far too much for her to bear, and indeed, she was quite miserable and homesick for some time.

To her surprise, though, her Aunt Hetty's sensible prediction that time would heal was in fact proving to be true. She had finally accepted the fact that, until her father's business problems were solved at home, she might just as well throw herself into the spirit of Avonlea. And thrown herself into it she had, becoming part of her dear mother's family, making friends and enjoying her new experiences as much as she could.

There were, however, some aspects of life in Avonlea that Sara could not, and would never, get used to. The sewing circle was one of them.

Sara hated sewing. In Montreal, she had never had to learn to sew. She remembered how she used to sit in the huge kitchen, munching on freshly baked cookies, happy in the company of the maids as they stitched and chattered. It had looked so deceptively simple. Beautiful lace bed linens, tablecloths and napkins were made or mended with care under the watchful eye of Nanny Louisa, who ran the household with the precision of a drill sergeant.

Sara knew that all the proper young ladies of Avonlea took great pride in their abilities with needle and thread, but she realized quite quickly that she herself was hopeless. What had seemed so easy for the servants back home in Montreal was an impossible task of coordination for Sara. Besides, she could never keep her mind on it. It was the sort of chore that begged to be accompanied by daydreams, and the more Sara let her imagination run away with her, the less she sewed.

There was another light knock at the door. Aunt Olivia poked her head in and smiled fondly at the lump in the bed. "Sara, rise and shine! You're missing a beautiful day."

Sara sighed. It was no use. The dream was gone. She peeked out from under the covers.

Her aunt looked as sunny as the morning itself. Her skin glowed with a dewy freshness and her eyes danced with the delight she took in the simplest of things. Her glossy, dark brown, upswept hair, with its becoming waves, gave her the look of a Gibson girl, Sara thought, just like the ones on the magazine covers in Montreal.

Olivia crossed the room and opened Sara's window, allowing fresh breezes to ruffle the lace curtains. "There now, maybe that will wake you up, lazybones," said Olivia.

Sara breathed deeply as the sweet air wafted through her room. She loved the smell of the apple blossoms from the neighboring King farm orchard. Quite suddenly, she found herself wondering if her mother had woken up on a morning just such as this one and smelled the same smells. Since this had once been her bedroom as well, Sara was quite sure she had. The thought made her feel close to her mother, even though she had died when Sara was only three. She wondered also if her mother had despised the thought of the sewing circle as much as she did.

"Did you have pleasant dreams?" her Aunt Olivia was asking, and Sara pulled herself from her reverie.

"I'm not sure you would call them pleasant," replied Sara thoughtfully, "but they were certainly interesting...what I can remember of them, that is." She paused and tried desperately to put the jigsaw puzzle of her dream back together. "Do you know, Aunt Olivia, I think I dreamt about Miss Cuthbert."

"Marilla?" asked Olivia. "Really?"

Sara swung her legs out of bed and stared out the window, her brow furrowed as she attempted to recall the fuzzy details. "She was standing all alone on the cliff, looking out to sea. She seemed very lonely. I called to her and..."

"And?" prompted Olivia.

"And someone knocked on my door and woke me up!" said Sara, with a wry smile.

"Well pardon me, madam!" teased Olivia, taking Sara's hands playfully and pulling her from the edge of the bed to her feet.

"Will Miss Cuthbert be at the sewing circle today?" Sara asked, as she and Olivia straightened the covers on her bed.

"I should think so," replied Olivia, "since Rachel is holding it at Green Gables."

"Good!" said Sara. "I should like to get to know Miss Cuthbert better. At least I can look forward to that, if nothing else."

Olivia looked sideways at Sara with a small smile on her face.

Chapter Two

"Only Providence knows why I take these things on, Marilla," huffed Rachel Lynde as she took yet another beautifully browned apple pie out of the oven in the kitchen at Green Gables.

Outside, Marilla Cuthbert gave the porch a few vigorous strokes with her broom. Try as she might, she could not ignore Rachel's voice as it carried through the kitchen window.

"Mind you," continued Rachel, oblivious to the fact that her audience of one was growing tired of her incessant flow of conversation, "things would be in a sorry state if I didn't. And I do find pleasure in the Avonlea sewing circle. Idle hands are not my cup of tea."

"Nor is an idle tongue," said Marilla, more to herself than anyone else.

Rachel Lynde had come to live at Green Gables after her husband Thomas died, and the two women were very dear friends, but there were times when Marilla felt that she would burst if she heard another righteous word from the dutiful Rachel.

Mrs. Lynde worked tirelessly to fill mission boxes, she was the head of the Women's Temperance League, she taught Sunday school and she ran the Avonlea sewing circle. However, she was one of those women who was not content to simply run her own life and be done with it. She felt duty-bound to inflict her capabilities and insights upon anyone who, to her way of thinking, didn't measure up.

"I just hope we can sew enough to fill a box for the rummage sale," said Rachel, bustling out the screen door backwards, carrying two more pies and setting them in the pie-cooler on the porch. "That Reverend Leonard has been worrying me about it for days. He should stick to preaching and leave the real work to those of us who know how to do it, that's what! Don't raise so much dust, Marilla. It'll stick to the pies!"

Marilla leaned wearily on her broom. "Really Rachel, do you think sewing will create the kind of appetite that warrants five pies?"

Rachel was astonished at Marilla's lack of observation and intuition. "I have seen several ladies of the sewing circle polish off half a pie at one sitting, Janet King in particular. Her daughter Felicity is going to be just like her, too. She's a pretty thing now, but dimples turn to fat over the years, that's what!" Rachel turned smartly and reentered the kitchen, letting the screen door slam behind her in her ample wake.

Marilla rolled her eyes. There was no arguing with Rachel. She sat down on one of the comfortable, old wicker chairs and attempted to adjust her mood. It really was a beautiful day. The red roses and pink clematis bloomed on the trellis surrounding the porch. There was a faint breeze that carried the undeniable scent of the sea. Marilla breathed deeply. The only sound that pierced the silence was the humming of the bees.

Slam! The screen door banged shut again. Marilla closed her eyes. Rachel obviously was not finished.

"Besides Marilla, the pies aren't all for the sewing circle. I've invited Alexander Abraham to tea tomorrow, so two of them are for him."

Ever since Rachel had made a friend of the reclusive, woman-hating curmudgeon Alexander Abraham, she had never let Marilla forget about it. She wore his friendship like a badge of honor.

Rachel looked at Marilla out of the corner of her eye. "I didn't think you'd mind, Marilla. A little male company would make a change around here. He asked me to his place first, but it is my experience that a woman is always in a stronger position if she is the one doing the asking. Of course," continued Rachel bluntly, "these are things beyond your understanding, Marilla."

Marilla tried to bite her tongue. It was a sore subject that she would just as soon not deal with.

Nevertheless, knowing the minute she opened her mouth it was a mistake, Marilla rose to the bait.

"Rachel, I lived with a man for fifty-odd years."

Rachel plunked herself into one of the wicker chairs, ready for a heart to heart chat.

"Dealing with a brother is in no way the same as dealing with a man. And of course, husbands are quite a different matter again....Poor Thomas, bless his soul."

Marilla did not deign not to reply, but she

could feel Rachel's eyes on her, and she knew that the subject was not closed.

"Marilla..." Rachel began, with that cautious tone that always preceded an out-and-out invasion of privacy. "If I may be so bold as to speak my mind, I've always wondered why you never did marry after you quarreled and broke it off with John Blythe?"

After a moment of silence, Marilla fastened her steely blue eyes on Rachel, who did not so much as flinch. "I hope the question has not caused you any sleepless nights, Rachel."

Not to be sidetracked, Rachel eagerly pursued her train of thought. "You weren't a bad-looking girl, and you had a passable personality. Why is it you never got a proposal?"

Marilla stirred uncomfortably in her chair, amazed once again by Rachel's unbelievable lack of tact. She felt an overwhelming need to put her in her place.

"If I may be permitted to speak *my* mind, Rachel, it's none of your affair."

For the first time, Rachel sensed a bit of pique on Marilla's part and was profoundly surprised.

"Well, no reason to get huffy Marilla, I'm sure. But you've missed out, that's what!"

"It has never worried me for a minute that I never married," said Marilla calmly.

"Well, maybe so, but it must have worried you that you never had the opportunity!" retorted Rachel.

Totally unaware of Marilla's barely controlled ire, Rachel was as smug as a bee full of nectar. She looked coyly at Marilla, becoming almost girlish.

"I might be getting mellow in my old age, but there is something comforting about having the attentions of a gentleman." She leaned forward conspiratorially. "Just between you and me, Marilla, I don't think it would take much to get Alexander Abraham to come courtin'."

Marilla looked as unimpressed as she felt and said dryly, "And what would you do if he did?"

With a self-satisfied smile on her face, Rachel folded her hands over her aproned lap. "Turn him down flat, that's what! Green Gables is my home now. I'm forever beholden to you for that. And you needn't worry, Marilla, I'll be here until the day they carry me out."

Marilla looked to Heaven and said, with thinly veiled sarcasm, "Well Rachel, that certainly sets my mind at ease."

Rachel smiled back at her friend, blissfully unaware of the emotions that she had stirred up.

Chapter Three

"Sara! Hurry yourself dear!" Olivia King rushed out the front door of Rose Cottage, carrying a sack of colorful remnants destined for the Avonlea sewing circle.

A very faint "I'm coming" floated through the screen door, but even from a distance, the note of reluctance was unmistakable. Olivia shook her head and smiled. She knew Sara was not looking forward to the afternoon. She was a child of many talents, but sewing, quite definitely, was not one of them.

The front door opened, but it was Hetty King who came through it, carrying her book. She sat down primly on her favorite chair and, without a word to Olivia, opened her text and proceeded to read. Olivia looked at her sister in surprise.

"Hetty! You're not ready!"

Without looking up, Hetty replied, "I'm not going."

"You always go to sewing circle," said a puzzled Olivia.

"Not when Rachel Lynde is holding it," replied Hetty, still not even looking up from her book.

The two sisters were as different as night and day. Olivia, the youngest member of the King tribe, wore her heart and dreams on her sleeve. She rushed headlong into life, and Hetty was forever chiding her to feel less and think more.

As the eldest of the Kings, Hetty prided herself on the fact that there was no nonsense about her. Her feet were planted firmly on the ground. She was as inscrutable as a statue, never allowing her true feelings to show if she could help it. Such a disposition served her well in her role as Avonlea's schoolmistress.

Olivia looked at her older sister and sighed. How exasperating Hetty could be at times!

"Hetty, you're being awfully pig-headed about something that happened between you and Rachel in grade seven. Just because she stole the affections of Romney Penhallow—"

Hetty had a long memory for insults or slights, and she never let go of a grudge.

"It wouldn't matter if it were yesterday!"

She looked up from her book, eyeing Olivia smartly. "Anyway, I'd rather collect for the rummage sale next week than listen to the sewing circle's endless prattle. I know the minute my back is turned they fasten onto me with their chatter."

Olivia tried to reason with her sister. "Now Hetty. You know that's not true." She took a deep breath and jumped into deep water. "Hetty, I don't usually interfere with your decisions, but I really—"

Hetty cut her off. "Then don't."

Sara appeared silently beside Olivia, and Hetty immediately turned her attention to her niece. Despite her outwardly cool disposition, a soft spot glowed in Hetty's heart for Sara.

Had anyone told her a year ago that she would find herself at the age of forty-seven looking after her dear departed sister Ruth's twelve-year-old daughter, she would have thought they were out of their minds. Now she couldn't for the life of her imagine what life would be like without Sara.

Her mind traveled back to that evening when Sara had first arrived at Rose Cottage with Nanny Louisa J. Banks, escaping the terrible scandal that arose when her father, Blair Stanley, was arrested for embezzling from his own company, Stanley Imports. She realized now, in her heart, that it was most unlikely that he was guilty as charged. However, until his court case was well and truly over, she knew that Sara was safe within the bosom of her mother's family on Prince Edward Island. When his troubles were over, then and only then would Hetty address the fact that Sara would most likely be expected to return to his side in Montreal.

Now Hetty looked at Sara appreciatively. She

never ceased to be amazed at the child's likeness to her sister Ruth. Poor dear Ruth, dead these nine years. She had been more than a sister to Hetty. Hetty, older by fifteen years, had almost raised Ruth. Losing her had felt almost like losing her own child. Hetty's eyes clouded over, but she blinked the tears rapidly away. Tarry not on the dead, but the living, she said to herself.

Sara was dressed beautifully in a spotless white eyelet-lace pinafore and a white hat adorned with spring flowers. Sara's anxious face betrayed her feelings. Like her Aunt Olivia's, Sara's moods were as easy to read as the book on her Aunt Hetty's lap.

Satisfied, Hetty nodded at her. "Now Sara, mind your manners, don't fidget and speak only when you're spoken to."

Sara's big blue eyes looked pleadingly at Hetty.

"Please Aunt Hetty, wouldn't it be better if I stayed home and helped you?"

"Helping me won't improve your sewing abilities," Hetty replied brusquely, adjusting Sara's sash.

"But I can't sew. Everyone will make fun of me," Sara said miserably.

"Watch Felicity. If you ask her nicely, she'll help you, I'm sure."

Hetty had just put into words the very thing that Sara detested and feared the most.

She rolled her eyes. "That would be a fate worse than death."

Sara's pretty cousin Felicity, Alec and Janet King's thirteen-year-old daughter, was the queen of domesticity. She was Miss Perfect, preparing herself for the role of the ideal mother and wife as described in the *Family Guide*, a book that she held in almost as much reverence as the Bible. She could sew and cook rings around Sara, and never let her forget it. The thought of turning to her for help was more than Sara could bear.

She caught her Aunt Olivia's eye. Olivia winked at her over Hetty's head, and that gave Sara some comfort.

Olivia made one last attempt.

"Hetty, I wish you'd come with us. I hate making excuses for you."

Hetty went back to her book. "You don't have to. Rachel will know why I'm not there. And rightly so."

Olivia sighed and picked up her sack, giving Sara her sewing kit to carry.

"Very well then. Come along Sara."

Sara followed her aunt slowly down the steps of Rose Cottage, meekly accepting her fate.

Chapter Four

The Avonlea sewing circle gathered in the cosy sitting room at Green Gables. This week's meeting was well attended by young and old alike. Very few people could say no to Rachel Lynde, whether motivated by friendship or the promise of a piece of one of her pies.

Nimble fingers were hard at work, sewing items of clothing for the rummage sale, as equally nimble tongues spread the latest gossip.

Sara made sure she sat as close to Marilla Cuthbert as possible, hoping for a chance to initiate a conversation with her, despite her Aunt Hetty's warnings to speak only when spoken to. To her dismay, her cousin Felicity had sat right beside her and was now sewing dutifully. Sara made a pretense of doing the same, looking sideways at her older cousin's handiwork with a mixture of admiration and jealousy.

Felicity was immaculate. Her chestnut curls shone from the one hundred brush strokes Felicity gave them faithfully each night. The ruffles on her white pinafore had been ironed to perfection and covered a new plaid dress that Sara had heard Felicity say she made herself. She was a pretty girl, Sara had to concede. She wished she had dimples like Felicity. Her Aunt Olivia was forever trying to fatten Sara up, but she was resigned to being as thin as a reed her entire life.

To Sara's relief, Felicity was on her best behavior, not once criticizing her attempts at a hemstitch. In fact, they were both uncharacteristically silent, trying to outdo each other in following the old edict of being seen and not heard. Though their tongues were still, however, their ears were wide open.

"I knew there'd be trouble when Tyrone Bell sold his place to a Yankee," Rachel Lynde was saying emphatically. "I don't know what Avonlea is coming to, with all these strange people rushing into it. Soon it won't be safe to sleep in our beds."

Sara giggled to herself as a sudden picture of Mrs. Lynde, guarding Green Gables in her nightcap, popped into her mind's eye. She had seen Mrs. Lynde in just such a state of dress when they had been quarantined at Alexander Abraham's. She felt sorry for any intruder who might be unlucky enough to encounter her. She was sure that such a sight would be enough to scare anyone away.

Mrs. Potts nodded her head knowingly at Rachel, her chins wobbling above her ample bosom. "Oh Rachel, I couldn't agree more about all these strangers."

Marilla looked up from her work and fixed her eyes on Mrs. Potts, a known busybody. "What other strangers are coming here, Mrs. Potts?"

There was nothing Mrs. Potts liked more than to pass along information, whether true or false.

"Haven't you heard? There's a family of Donnells, for one thing. They belong down East and nobody knows anything about them."

"And that shiftless Timothy Cotton family are coming up from White Sands, and they'll simply be a burden on the public," said Rachel with finality from across the room. "He's the one who's consumptive—"

"When he isn't stealing," added Mrs. Potts, safe in the knowledge of her own spotless reputation.

Mrs. Lawson did not share Mrs. Potts's mean-spirited zest for gossip, but running the general store with her husband put her in the enviable position of being at the center of Avonlea's news, and she could hold her own with the best of them in passing it on.

"I heard Paul Irving is coming from the States to live with his grandmother," she said between stitches. "You remember his father, Rachel? Stephen Irving?"

Rachel searched hungrily through her memory.

"Oh, isn't he the one that jilted Lavender Lewis over in Grafton?"

"I don't think he jilted her. There was a quarrel. I suppose there was blame on both sides," said a very diplomatic Mrs. Lawson.

"Well, anyway, he never married her, and she's been as queer as possible ever since," said Rachel, and many of the ladies nodded their heads in agreement. Poor Lavender Lewis had been the source of countless conversations at the sewing circle.

Mrs. Potts suddenly remembered a tidbit she had saved for the occasion. "Have you heard? Amy Peters is back from the West, came last week, and..." she said, pausing to make sure her audience gave her the silence she expected, "...and she's going to marry a Winnipeg millionaire! You may be sure her mother lost no time in telling it far and wide." She narrowed her eyes gleefully as her comment received the reaction she had hoped for.

Rachel shook her head in disbelief. "Amy's a nice enough girl, but she's not in the millionaire class."

Mrs. Potts looked up at her daughter. "My Sally saw Amy Peters the other day, didn't you, Sally?"

Sally Potts, her mouse-brown hair freshly out

of papers so that it resembled a collection of corkscrews, looked up from where she sat, which was as far away from Sara and Felicity as possible. Ever since the magic lantern show, when Sara had exposed Sally as the instigator behind Jasper Dale's humiliation and the Town Hall fire, Sally had treated Sara and the rest of the King children with a new, if distant, respect. It had taken a dunking in the bloodsucker-filled creek, however, to bring her to this new state. Sara smiled to herself as she thought about it. It had been a mean thing to do, but no one was more deserving than Sally.

Sally Potts had inherited her mother's talent for gossip, and she entered into the conversation enthusiastically.

"Her beau has simply showered her with jewelry. Her engagement ring is a huge diamond cluster."

"Probably looks like a plaster on Amy's fat paw," added Mrs. Potts, her body shaking with laughter.

The women couldn't help but join her, tittering behind the handkerchiefs they were sewing, looking slightly guilty at their irreverence to the poor, absent Amy. Sara noticed that Marilla Cuthbert was the notable exception to the general frivolity, and her disapproving glance in Mrs.

Potts's direction put a damper on even that lady's mirth.

Sensing a need for a change of subject, Mrs. Lawson smiled charmingly at her hostess.

"Speaking of beaux, Rachel, what's all this I hear about you and Alexander Abraham?"

Sara had not realized the sewing circle could be so entertaining, and her mood had vastly improved. Her eyes twinkled, and she couldn't help but give Felicity a tiny nudge in the ribs with her elbow.

Rachel's back stiffened. She did not quite like this turn of conversation, but she was determined to set the record straight.

"There's nothing to hear! We're friends. Nothing more than that! I shall always be faithful to my late husband's memory. Excuse me!" She suddenly felt the need to see to the tea kettle in the kitchen. A dozen pairs of eyes watched her go.

Mrs. Potts leaned towards Marilla and whispered in her ear. "Well Marilla, if you ask me, there's more between them than a friendship!"

Marilla looked uncomfortable. "What do you mean, Mrs. Potts?"

"I suppose you'd miss her company if it came to anything," mused Mrs. Potts aloud. "Mind you, at your age, I'm sure you're used to being on your own."

Marilla's mood had gone steadily downhill since her conversation with Rachel that morning, and Mrs. Potts was not improving it one bit. She tried desperately to consider the source of such a ridiculous statement, but her annoyance got the better of her.

"If people could stitch as easily as they talk, Mrs. Potts, the sewing circle would be a very productive group indeed."

Mrs. Potts raised her eyebrows in amusement at Marilla's severity, and she looked around the group with an exaggerated chastened smirk.

Sara leaned over and whispered to Felicity, "Even *my* imagination would have to stretch to think of Mrs. Lynde and Mr. Abraham as beaux."

Felicity started to giggle at the thought, and they were immediately chided by Olivia.

"Now Sara, mind what Hetty said. You're here to sew, not talk. And a hemstitch is not supposed to look like that."

Olivia took Sara's crumpled piece of cloth away from her and started to correct it, but Sara's thoughts were on other, much more important things than stitches and hems. She looked at her Aunt Olivia admiringly. She really was beautiful. Her dark hair framed her perfectly heart-shaped face. Her long lashes cast dainty shadows on her high cheekbones. Sara wondered how many hearts her aunt had broken. No sooner had she thought about it than she had to know.

"I'll bet you had lots of beaux, didn't you, Aunt Olivia?" Sara said, a little louder than she had meant to, and suddenly the room was silent.

A rose blush started to creep up Olivia's cheeks. "Oh my! Not really...just one..." she said hesitantly.

Mrs. Potts didn't miss a beat. "Oh yes. Edwin Clarke, wasn't it Olivia? Hetty sent him packing. Evidently a Clarke wasn't good enough for a King. Hetty always did set herself above everyone else."

Rachel returned from the kitchen to catch this last comment and said wryly, "That's just one of her faults. No wonder she lost Romney Penhallow."

Olivia flushed and sewed furiously.

Sara sat quite still, her eyes wide with the discovery of this new information. She never ceased to be amazed at all the secrets that grown-ups were capable of keeping. Imagine! Her Aunt Hetty interfering in Aunt Olivia's affairs of the heart. How dreadful! She wondered what the reason could possibly have been. Aunt Hetty was strict, but she always wanted the best for Olivia.

Mrs. Lawson looked teasingly at Janet King.

"Janet, you were the one with all the beaux."

Janet blushed like a schoolgirl, not completely displeased. "Oh now...I might have had a few...." Sara and Felicity looked at each other with anticipation.

"A few?" Rachel snorted. "Janet King, you threw yourself at every available male for miles! It's a good thing Alec King caught you, or you might have ended up with one of the Sloane boys."

Rachel, having hit her target, swept off to bring yet more plates of delicacies to the dining table.

Janet's smile faded, and she shifted self-consciously in her chair, casting a glance at Felicity, hoping beyond hope that her daughter had missed Mrs. Lynde's words.

But Felicity was on the edge of her seat. "Really mother? You've never told us about any beaux!"

Her mother gave her a brittle smile. "Mrs. Lynde is exaggerating a great deal. I had one or two beaux before your father. That's all."

Sara glanced across the room at Marilla Cuthbert. Why had she not been taking part in the banter? Sara realized with a start that the expression on Miss Cuthbert's face was very like the one she had worn in her dream, lonely and left out. Sara felt a sudden rush of sympathy. She remembered that dreadful, empty feeling she herself had when she first arrived in Avonlea. She was determined to include Miss Cuthbert in the conversation, Sara asked in her clear, ringing voice.

"Did you ever have a beau, Miss Cuthbert?"

A silence fell over the room. Even Rachel, carrying a stack of plates, stopped in her tracks and looked from Sara to Marilla. Sara felt her Aunt Olivia nudging her. "Sara, really..."

A change came over Marilla's face, but she said nothing. Rachel, as usual, tried to fill in the silence.

"Well, Sara Stanley, Marilla has had a real sensible life. She didn't have time nor temperament for beaux, did you Marilla?"

Marilla's face was a study of failing self-control. To her dying day, she would never know what possessed her to do what she did in the next minute. Perhaps all the prickles and stings and slurs she had endured on account of never having had a beau had a cumulative effect, and it all came to a head then and there.

An expression of near defiance took the place of embarrassment. "I had one once," she replied to Sara's question.

Every woman in the room stopped sewing and looked at Marilla.

"Oh well, we all know about John Blythe,

Marilla," began Rachel. "But of course nothing much came of that. And as I was just saying this morning—"

"I'm not talking about John Blythe, Rachel." Marilla had, in fact, meant John Blythe, but Rachel had stolen her thunder, pushing her further over the line.

"Then who *are* you talking about, Marilla?" Rachel pursued.

"Yes, who was it?" asked an excited Sara. The room was all ears, and Sara glowed with anticipation. Her special interest in Marilla Cuthbert seemed to be justified.

"Won't you tell us about him?" coaxed Felicity.

"Yes, Marilla. Tell us. We're all interested," said Mrs. Lawson, wholesomely sincere.

"It's news to us that you ever had a romantic attachment," said Mrs. Potts with a nasty little laugh. She and Rachel Lynde exchanged significant smiles.

If Mrs. Potts had not said that, in that way, Marilla might have returned to her usual good sense. But she had said it, and Marilla knew there was no turning back. In for a penny, in for a pound.

Every last member of the sewing circle craned forward to listen as Marilla opened her mouth to speak.

"Nobody here knew anything about him. I

met him when I was visiting my Aunt Tilly in
Blakely, New Brunswick."

"Now when would that be, Marilla?" asked
Mrs. Lawson.

"It was a long time ago," replied Marilla quietly.

Mrs. Potts winked at Mrs. Lawson. "Oh, that's
a likely story Marilla. Can't you be more specific?"

Mrs. Lawson looked genuinely puzzled. "I
can't remember the last time you were away from
Avonlea. How old were you?"

Marilla swallowed and replied, "I was...
twenty-eight."

Rachel considered this new information slowly.

"Well, I do remember you making that trip,
but you certainly never said anything about
having a beau...."

Sara, who had been trying to get a word in edge-
wise, took advantage of Rachel Lynde's sudden
silence. "What was his name, Miss Cuthbert?" she
asked excitedly.

"Duncan," Marilla replied promptly, off the top
of her head. It had always been her favorite name.

"Duncan who?" Sara wanted to know.

For a dreadful moment, Marilla's mind went
completely blank, but then she spied a newspaper
on the table beside her, open to an advertisement
for "McTavish Porous Plasters."

"McTavish...Duncan McTavish." The two

names were joined in sudden and irrevocable matrimony.

"Oh really?" said Mrs. Potts, not convinced.

"That's the first I've heard of it," said Rachel.

"What was he like?" prompted Sara.

"He was...from a good family, honest, hard-working...upright..." began Marilla. Neither Sara nor Felicity was interested, however, in such fundamental good qualities.

"But was he handsome?" Felicity wanted to know.

Sara's eyes lit up with imagination. "I'll bet he was tall and dark, with a straight nose and a strong chin...just like a hero out of a book. I'm sure he told you that your skin was like cream, and your eyes were the color of cornflowers."

Marilla looked sternly at Sara over the top of her glasses. "No, Sara Stanley, he said no such thing."

"Well, why didn't you marry him, Miss Cuthbert?" Felicity had had enough of Sara's musings. She wanted to get to the point.

Mrs. Potts was glad someone had finally asked the question. "Yes, Marilla. Tell us why you didn't."

Marilla was caught slightly off guard, but recovered herself. "It was impossible...there were...differences," she said abruptly, busying herself once again with her sewing.

"What do you mean?" asked Sara, gently.

"He was...a Methodist," said Marilla. Rachel looked at Marilla in shock. She could not have been more surprised if Marilla had said he was a bigamist.

"A Methodist? Well, no wonder you never mentioned him, Marilla. You can move Heaven and Earth but Providence knows you can't bring a Methodist and a Presbyterian together."

For the first time that day, Marilla quietly blessed Rachel's narrow-mindedness and pursued her story with new vigor.

"I tried to explain that to him, but he wouldn't accept it as a reason, and we quarreled. So I left Blakely. I told him that I had an obligation to my aged parents, and it wasn't fair to leave my brother Matthew alone with them." Marilla bowed her head sadly over her sewing.

"Oh, Miss Cuthbert!" Sara's eyes grew misty. "How utterly devastating. Whatever happened to him?"

Marilla avoided her eyes. "He went out West and I haven't heard anything from him since. I don't even know if he's alive or dead."

The women digested all they had heard, and Marilla, to tell the dreadful truth, had almost enjoyed herself. There was a new respect dawning in people's eyes. Henceforth she would be a woman with a romantic past, a very different thing from an old maid who had never had a beau.

Rachel broke the silence. "Well, of all the things there ever were or will be! It's a mystery to me how you managed to keep this to yourself all these years, Marilla."

"Now isn't that just like you?" remarked Mrs. Potts, snapping a thread between her teeth for punctuation.

"Well, it didn't seem to be of importance," said Marilla.

"Not important! A suitor from your past!" burst out Sara, despite another warning nudge from her Aunt Olivia.

"Well, this is something new in my experience," said Rachel, shaking herself into action by serving the tea and pies. "Tea's served, ladies. And I've made my famous apple pies. Help yourselves."

Marilla breathed a sigh of relief as all the ladies rose and approached the tea table. Janet King was first in line. Rachel eyed Janet, satisfied that she was correct in her assessment of the sewing circle's appetite and, in particular, Janet's. "Oh, take a bigger piece than that, Janet King!" she chided. "It'll save you coming back for more."

Sara watched as Marilla buried her head in

her sewing. She had a sudden impulse to go over and give her a comforting hug, but something about Marilla's demeanor made her think twice. Instead, she joined Felicity on her way to the refreshment table. Sewing circle was not nearly as dreadful as she had expected it to be.

Rachel Lynde also had her eye on Marilla.

She was not one to miss much, and she watched as her old friend took off her glasses and wiped her eyes wearily. Something was not quite right here, and Rachel meant to find out just what it was.

Chapter Five

As was usual in a small village like Avonlea, news as exciting as Marilla Cuthbert's revelation did not rest within the confines of the sewing circle. No indeed. It was a morsel that kept Mrs. Potts and Mrs. Lawson well occupied on their long walk home, all the way from Green Gables to the Lawson general store.

"To my mind, the only man other than John Blythe who ever said boo to Marilla Cuthbert was George Maybrick," said Mrs. Potts, with a furrowed brow.

"Really?" replied Mrs. Lawson, trying to recall

if she had ever heard that particular gentleman's name before.

"Mind you, he ended up with Flora Dumstead," said Mrs. Potts, with a sideways look to her companion that intimated the man's judgment was far from sound.

"You don't say," said Mrs. Lawson, who was beginning to feel a little overwhelmed by all the information she had had to digest that day.

"She was cross-eyed and redheaded, so it shows how dubious his taste was," said Mrs. Potts matter-of-factly, nodding with satisfaction at her assessment.

"Well, it was all before my time," said Mrs. Lawson, with a lack of diplomacy unusual for her.

Mrs. Potts's previously friendly demeanor became icy. Any reference to her age generally had that effect.

"Before mine, too, my dear, but it's common knowledge," she snapped. "Good day to you!"

"Good day to you, Mrs. Potts," said poor Mrs. Lawson, realizing, too late, her faux pas.

Mrs. Potts turned and swept down the main street of Avonlea in full sail. Mrs. Lawson sighed. Mrs. Potts was a very good customer, and she knew the general store would suffer greatly for the next week or so.

Mrs. Lawson's thoughts were disturbed by

Mrs. Biggins, the owner of the rooming house next door, who leaned over her white picket fence with a look of barely controlled glee on her face and called to Mrs. Lawson, "What's all this I hear about Marilla Cuthbert?"

Mrs. Lawson joined her neighbor at her fence. "Well, I'm not one to wag my tongue," she said quietly, looking over her shoulder. "But I must admit, I've been taken by surprise. The sewing circle was anything but dull today, Mrs. Biggins."

Mrs. Biggins leaned forward encouragingly, and Mrs. Lawson caught her up on the events of the afternoon.

The news spread like wildfire through the sleepy village. Not long after her conversation with Mrs. Lawson, Mrs. Biggins arrived at the field her husband was plowing and surprised him with a picnic lunch. She generally only did this sort of thing on the good man's birthday, but she couldn't wait for suppertime to tell him such a delicious piece of news.

"You don't say!" was Ira Biggins's reaction, between mouthfuls. "You mean that holier-than-thou Marilla Cuthbert has kept this to herself all these years?"

"I couldn't believe it myself. But Mrs. Lawson is not one to tell tales, and besides, she was there! She heard it with her own ears." Mrs. Biggins screwed her face up with concentration. "I think she said Marilla jilted him at the altar."

Mr. Biggins shook his head and took another bite of his bread and cheese.

At the King farm, the pastoral calm of the orchard in full bloom was broken by an indignant Janet King, whose feathers were still ruffled by the events of the sewing circle.

Alec King, repairing the buggy listened with amusement as his wife poured out her grievances.

"That Rachel Lynde! I could have boxed her ears. Imagine saying those things about me in front of all those people, including my own daughter. I was mortified!" Janet's usually flushed face was even pinker at the memory of it all.

Alec glanced at his fuming wife with a twinkle in his eye. "Sounds to me like I'm a lucky man to have lured you away from all those admirers."

"Don't you believe a word of that gossip, Alec King!" said Janet briskly, turning her back on him to hide her smile of pleasure.

Alec gave her shoulder a squeeze and whispered in her ear, "I must admit that I find the fact that you had a few beaux before me more believable than Marilla Cuthbert's confession of having a past."

Janet whirled around in amazement. "How did you know that?" she demanded.

"Heard it in town," said Alec, going back to his work. "You know how people talk, buzzing like bees in a hive."

Janet shook her head and looked thoughtful. "I don't know what to think on that score. It certainly did come out of the blue." Her eyes took on the misty look of the hopelessly romantic. "It's strange but I hope it's true."

"Hmmm?" said Alec, tightening a bolt on one of the buggy wheels.

Janet looked at him with affection. "Well, everyone needs a little romance in their lives." She leaned down and gave Alec a quick, uncharacteristic kiss and hurried away.

Chapter Six

The grown-ups of Avonlea were not the only ones chattering that afternoon. Under the spreading boughs of an old apple tree sat Felicity, her younger sister Cecily and Sara, all diligently sewing. All but Sara, that is.

Sara's eyes shone as she caught Cecily up on the events of the afternoon. Cecily listened eagerly, her long, flaxen braids bobbing every time she nodded encouragement to Sara to continue.

Ten-year-old Cecily couldn't wait to be old

enough to be accepted into the mysteries of the sewing circle, but her cousin Sara could tell a story so well it was almost like being there.

Felicity listened with mounting annoyance, her nose out of joint at her little sister's obvious attentiveness to Sara. "Sara Stanley," she said haughtily, "you shouldn't gossip so much."

"There is a great difference between gossip and factual reporting, Felicity King!" retorted Sara.

"You should be concentrating on your hem-stitch," muttered Felicity.

Felicity had still not entirely come to terms with Sara's sudden arrival in Avonlea and her inclusion in the bosom of the King family. She had always enjoyed a certain amount of power as the eldest of the King children, and Sara was an unwanted rival in this respect. Not able to match Sara's innate intelligence and wit, Felicity was content to lord it over her in the domestic arena. At the sewing circle, where Felicity could reign supreme, all was well between the two girls. But here on King ground, when Sara appeared to be monopolizing her little sister's affections—that was another matter entirely.

Sara looked down at her crumpled piece of cloth. She had indeed forgotten all about her promise to Aunt Hetty to finish the handkerchief she had started at the sewing circle. But how

could anyone even begin to think about hem-
stitches in the face of such a tragedy of the heart?
She sighed and attempted to get her needle and
thread to do what they ought to do, but her imagination would not rest.

"Wouldn't it be romantic if Mr. Duncan
McTavish returned and swept Marilla Cuthbert
away after so many years of pining for a lost
love?"

"That's unlikely to happen, and anyway, he'd
still be a Methodist," said the ever-practical Felicity,
straightening her perfect needlework and looking
at it critically.

At that moment their older cousin Andrew
came towards them, pushing a wheelbarrow in
which Felicity's younger brother Felix sat, hap-
pily munching on an apple. Felicity didn't mind
the thought of Andrew's company. At thirteen,
he was old enough to behave agreeably most of
the time, and besides, Felicity always felt that he
had somewhat of a crush on her, even though he
never dared show it. This unfounded certainty
raised Andrew to a higher level in Felicity's
eyes.

Eleven-year-old Felix, on the other hand, was
the bane of her existence. He was a known mis-
chief-maker. Wherever he went, trouble just naturally followed. His twinkling eyes and infectious

smile, however, usually saved him from the full consequences of his actions. Felicity rolled her eyes. Just when things were relatively calm and quiet....

Sara was oblivious to their comings and goings. Her mind was in Blakely, New Brunswick.

"Just think, Miss Cuthbert's life, changed..." she groped for just the right word, "...ir-re-vocally!" she finished with triumph.

"*Irrevocably!*" piped up cousin Andrew.

Andrew's father was a geologist presently stationed in South America. Andrew had inherited his father's thirst for knowledge. Of all the King family, he was the one who most often had his head in a book, and he never lost a chance to utilize the knowledge he gleaned from his studies.

"Irrevocably," repeated Sara correctly, annoyed at the interruption to her thoughts. "Her life was changed irrevocably...." She paused, and Andrew nodded. "Just because she was born a Presbyterian and he was born a Methodist. Sometimes I think that religion is more trouble than it's worth!"

Cecily was shocked to the depths of her innocent soul. "Sara Stanley! You can't mean that!"

"I do mean it," said Sara emphatically. "Tell me," she challenged the others. "What is the difference between a Presbyterian and a Methodist?"

"There's a great deal of a difference. Everyone knows that!" said an indignant Felicity, supreme in the knowledge that her family belonged to the right church.

"Methodists say 'amen' a whole lot more than Presbyterians do!" said Felix, adding his two cents to the conversation. The other children just looked at him. Felicity rolled her eyes in disgust.

"I've heard them!" he insisted. "They do!"

"That's still not reason enough not to marry one of them," said Sara, picking up her sewing to signal the end of the subject.

Felicity was not quite willing to let Sara have the last word. "You'll never marry either, Sara, if you can't sew a straight line. No man will have you," she commented.

"Any man who would only marry me for my sewing is not worth anything anyway, Felicity King," retorted Sara. "You can have him."

"I pity the man who gets you, Felicity," said Felix, chortling to himself.

Felicity looked daggers at him. "Not half so much as I pity the poor wretched girl who says yes to you," she said.

Felix wrinkled his nose at her. "I'd never marry anyone with a tongue like yours. One of these days you're gonna choke on it. That's what mother says."

Sara giggled quietly to herself. Felicity glared at her for taking Felix's side. She pursed her lips, trying to think of a retort that would put her younger cousin properly in her place. Instead, she fastened her eyes on the crumpled piece of material that Sara was painstakingly working on, and snatched it away from her.

"What are you doing, Sara? You still don't know how to do a hemstitch!"

Sara rolled her eyes.

"Here, let me show you," continued an imperious Felicity. She held the piece of cloth gingerly between two fingers and looked at it disparagingly. "What is this thing anyway?"

"It's a handkerchief," replied Sara, through gritted teeth.

"Something like this will never sell in the rummage sale. It looks like it's already been used. Your hem's not even straight."

Sara had reached the end of her patience. "Give it back!" she demanded.

Felicity smirked and coolly handed the offending item over.

Chapter Seven

That night, on the moonlit porch of Green Gables, the lulling drone of the tree toads and the crickets could bring no peace to Marilla Cuthbert as she rocked back and forth in her favorite chair, her head full of her own thoughts.

An owl hooted for its mate in the distance. The screen door squeaked and then banged shut. Rachel lowered herself into a rocker and sat for a rare silent moment, observing Marilla from the shadows. For a few moments, she struggled with herself, opening her mouth to speak, then quickly shutting it again. Finally, however, she convinced herself of her duty to speak her mind.

"I must say, Marilla, that was a pretty astonishing revelation you made this afternoon. Especially considerin' our talk this morning. If I didn't know you for the sensible person you are, I'd say there was fancy in there somewheres."

Marilla continued to rock, but so quietly that, for a moment, Rachel thought she might be asleep. She was almost startled when Marilla's deep voice broke the silence.

"You know, Rachel, everyone in Avonlea thinks they know every little bit about everyone else, but there are some things, I'm sure even about you, that people do not know."

Rachel moved forward in her chair to refute this, but Marilla went on.

"If there was anything about your present situation with Alexander Abraham that you would like to keep to yourself, I would be bound to honor that, and I would hope you would do the same for me."

"You can be sure *I* have nothing to hide, Marilla," said a complacent Rachel.

Marilla turned and gave Rachel a piercing glance. "Goodnight Rachel," she said. Then she rose wearily and went into the house, uncharacteristically letting the door slam behind her.

Rachel jumped at the unexpected noise and then sat and stared out into the night in stunned silence. "Just when you think you know someone." She shook her head slowly and looked up at the moon. "You're never safe from surprises till you're dead!"

Inside, Marilla herself started nervously as the door slammed. Then she moved heavily towards the stairs leading to the second floor of Green Gables. As she passed by a mirror she paused, and sadly shook her head at her reflection.

Her mother's words, long forgotten, floated through her mind, unbidden. "Oh what a tangled web we weave, when first we practise to deceive."

She sighed and continued on her way up the stairs. It was all very well to be in for a pound as a penny, but what would the real cost be?

Chapter Eight

The morning sun streamed through the window of the kitchen in Rose Cottage. Peter Craig, the hired boy, clattered through the screen door from the back porch and noisily dropped a load of kindling into the wood box next to the stove. Last-minute baking for the rummage sale filled the air with the heavenly scent of raisins and cinnamon and fresh bread. Peter took an appreciative sniff and, pushing his sandy hair out of his eyes, he spied some blueberry muffins sitting on the counter to cool. He looked around. Sara was sitting with her back to him, hunched over the kitchen table. He called a good morning greeting to her and was answered by a barely audible mumur. He shrugged, surveyed the territory once again, grabbed one of the muffins and made his escape out the screen door.

All the sunshine and pleasant aromas in the world could not have lifted Sara's spirits, however, as she sat needle and thread in hand, attempting to finish the hem on the same hand-

cхcхcхcх

If Mrs. Potts had not said that,
in that way, Marilla might have returned to her usual
good sense. But she had said it, and Marilla knew
there was no turning back.
In for a penny, in for a pound.

❦❦❦

"Wouldn't it be romantic if Mr. Duncan McTavish
returned and swept Marilla Cuthbert away after so
many years of pining for a lost love?"
"That's unlikely to happen, and anyway, he'd still be a
Methodist," said the ever-practical Felicity,
straightening her perfect needlework
and looking at it critically.

∾

As Rachel observed these two people talking
and chuckling together, she was suddenly
struck with the horror of realization.
She had doubted Marilla, her best friend on this earth,
when obviously everything Marilla had said about
Duncan McTavish was quite true.

❦❦❦❦❦

"Thank you, Mr. McTavish," said Marilla,
in her low voice, as clear as a bell.
"A fine day, isn't it?" remarked Mr. McTavish as he
took his place beside her.
"One to remember," she said as she flashed him
a brilliant smile.

kerchief that had haunted her since the sewing circle.

"Ouch!" Sara exclaimed, and sucked on her wounded finger.

Aunt Hetty whisked into the room for her wicker basket, which was filled with supplies. She paused at the rack of blueberry muffins, counting them with a puzzled look on her face. She looked at Sara's back and smiled knowingly. Good, she thought, she could use a little meat on her bones. She collected up the rest of the muffins and placed them carefully in a napkin in her basket.

"Sara, I have to help Aunt Janet set up the tea table for the rummage sale, so I'll be leaving now. You come along with Olivia."

Hetty glanced at Sara, expecting at least some response. When there was none, her eyes fell on the pitiful square of cotton clutched awkwardly in Sara's hand. She replaced the basket on the counter with a thump.

"Oh Sara, didn't you learn anything at that sewing circle, child?" she asked with exasperation, taking a better look at her niece's handiwork. "No, look," she said impatiently, taking the needle and thread from Sara's hand. "This is the way you do the cross-stitch!" She screwed up her face in distaste. "There...and there and there," said Hetty, her fingers picking away at the stitches like a chicken pecking for grain in a barnyard.

Sara watched in exasperation. "You'll have to rip out all those stitches along the edge and start again," said Hetty with finality.

Sara stared at the ceiling, counting to ten in her mind. Hetty glanced at her watch in despair at the passing of time and picked up her basket once again.

"Now then! I'll see you there. And mind you're not late! And wear your hat! Olivia!" she called up the stairs, "Sara will be coming with you!" Then out she flew.

Sara took a deep breath and grabbed the pair of scissors that lay beside her on the table. She gingerly poked at the offending stitches with the sharpest point of the blade. The stitches stubbornly held. Losing her patience, Sara stabbed angrily at the material. There was the unmistakable sound of ripping cloth, and Sara gasped as she stared at the sudden gaping hole right in the middle of her handkerchief.

Olivia's voice reached her from the hallway.

"Sara, I'll just fix my hat and pick up a few more things and then we'll go."

Sara looked frantically around, trying to decide what to do. Her aunt's approaching footsteps spurred her on and within seconds she had stuffed the dreadful handkerchief deep into the wood box beside the stove, grabbed her hat and disappeared out the back door.

"Ready, Sara?" called Olivia as she entered the kitchen. Puzzled, she looked around at the empty room. "That's funny. I thought she was coming with me!"

Chapter Nine

A breeze fragrant with apple blossoms wafted through the King orchard as Olivia made her way towards the town, swinging her basket with the exuberance of a girl. She turned when she heard the sound of running feet coming from behind her, fully expecting to see Sara. It was Cecily, however, her face wreathed in smiles, her braids bouncing as she ran. Felicity followed at a more sedate pace.

"Aunt Olivia! Wait up! Look what I brought!" Cecily proudly held out a basket covered in a sparkling white doily. "Some cinnamon buns to sell at the rummage sale! I made them myself!"

"With my help," added Felicity smugly.

"Don't they look nice," said Olivia, ignoring Felicity's remark and admiring Cecily's baking. "Do you think I could get a penny apiece for them?" Cecily wanted to know as they continued on their walk.

"Oh, I'm sure you will," replied Olivia, fondly ruffling Cecily's bangs.

Not to be outdone, Felicity took her handiwork from her basket to show her aunt. "I'm going to charge ten cents apiece for my serving napkins."

"Well, you can try," replied Olivia, wondering to herself when, if ever, Felicity would grow out of her need to better everyone else. Much as she loved her niece, she found it more than a little annoying. "Have you seen Sara?" she asked, to change the subject. "She was supposed to help me this morning, but she disappeared right after breakfast and I haven't seen hide nor hair of her since."

"Well, I haven't seen her," said Felicity. "Mind you, if her handiwork hasn't improved since I last saw it, she's probably too embarrassed to show her face."

Olivia rolled her eyes. "Felicity," she admonished. "Try to be a little more charitable!"

Chapter Ten

At the very moment that inquiries about her whereabouts were being posed, Sara Stanley was thoroughly enjoying herself. Her mood had improved significantly from the moment she had rid herself of the annoying responsibility of sewing. She had taken the back route to town through the woods, delighting in the scent of the pines and the feel of the springy moss beneath her feet. She intended to follow the path to the village, and as quickly as she could, head off through the fields and down the slope to the dunes of the beach. It wouldn't do to be seen anywhere near the Town Hall. She had no intention of being hauled into that rummage sale.

The bright sunshine at the end of the path hailed the woods' end and Sara found herself emerging in a clearing behind the Biggins' boarding house. She skipped along the main street of Avonlea, relishing the fact that it was quite deserted, everyone being in attendance at the rummage sale.

As she approached Lawson's general store, she was delighted to see something quite out of the ordinary. A colorful, almost Gypsy-like buggy stood there, green with bright red wheels, decorated with lavish white lettering and illustrations. She hadn't meant to tarry, but this was far too interesting not to investigate. As she moved closer, she was able to make out what was written on the side of it.

"MCTAVISH POROUS PLASTERS" it proclaimed. "Cures all ailments and complaints!"

Sara looked at the pictures on the buggy with fascination. The medical-style illustrations showed smiling patients applying the plasters to their shoulders and chests. Suddenly, the familiar voice of Mr. Lawson reached her from the other side of the buggy. Sara peeked around the side, unnoticed.

Mr. Lawson was shaking hands with a man on the porch of the general store, a stranger, for Sara had never set eyes on him before. He was tall, well dressed and impressive in appearance, even though she guessed that he must be quite a bit older, in his fifties or even his early sixties.

"Thank you for the space outside your store, Mr. Lawson," said the man, as Sara watched, out of sight.

"Well, good luck to you, sir, but my customers seem to prefer the old fashioned remedies. Mustard plasters! They swear by them, Mr. McTavish," said a smiling Mr. Lawson.

Sara frowned slightly as she heard the stranger's last name.

"But porous plasters are revolutionary, Mr. Lawson. And please, call me Duncan."

Sara's mouth fell open. Duncan! She almost said it aloud. Duncan! Duncan McTavish!

"And believe me, I know all about Easterners and their ways," continued the stranger. "My family's roots are in the East."

"You don't say!" replied Mr. Lawson. "Where abouts?"

"New Brunswick," said Duncan McTavish, and Sara's mouth dropped even further.

"But, I must admit, the West has won me over."

Mr. Lawson shook his head in admiration. "Well, it requires a certain breed to go out West."

"Oh, I don't know," said Mr. McTavish. "Being a bachelor makes it easier, Mr. Lawson. But a good businessman like yourself would do well, family or no family."

Mr. Lawson stroked his chin self-consciously at the praise and turned towards his store proudly.

In doing so he caught sight of Sara peeking around the side of Mr. McTavish's buggy.

"Sorry Sara, I didn't see you there. Can I help you with something?"

Sara, totally speechless, stared first at Mr. Lawson, and then at the stranger, and finally took off at a run down the street.

Mr. Lawson turned to Duncan McTavish. "Kids!" he said, shaking his head, and the two men chuckled.

Chapter Eleven

The Avonlea Town Hall was buzzing with the sounds of commerce and scuttlebutt as women, men and children sampled and bought, tasted and tattled, all in the name of the mission that would be the sole receipient of their honorable charity.

Hetty and Janet King held court at the tea table, which was laden with little cakes and delicacies of all shapes, sizes and colors, the result of many hours of labor in the kitchens of Avonlea. Hetty watched with some disapproval as her sister-in-law Janet sampled more than her share of the sweets.

Cecily stood proudly by her cinnamon buns, waiting for her first customer.

At the linen table, Felicity folded her serving napkins just so and displayed them conspicuously among the other contributions.

Reverend Leonard passed through the crowd, sampling a piece of pie here, nodding appreciatively at handiwork there, congratulating everyone on their generous donations. He assured them that their unselfish efforts would certainly lighten the sorrowful state of the less fortunate and the needy.

Over by the preserves and jam table, the chatter was definitely not focused on the plight of the less fortunate.

"Well, mind you, I wasn't there," said Mrs. Biggins in a low voice. "But Mrs. Lawson told me all about it. I must say, we have underestimated Marilla all these years. It just goes to show that we mustn't judge people by their outsides."

Mrs. Potts rolled her eyes knowingly. "If you ask me, the whole thing is more than a little fishy."

"Why do you say that, Mrs. Potts?" asked Mrs. Lawson's niece, a naive girl of sixteen.

"Yes, what makes you say that?" queried Mrs. Lawson coolly, still irked by Mrs. Potts's boycott of her store as a result of their exchange some days before.

Mrs. Potts looked at Mrs. Lawson and smiled one of her slow, irritating smiles. "My sister-in-law grew up in Blakely, New Brunswick, and she says the only McTavish she remembers was an old maiden lady with no family."

There was a moment of silence as the full import of this statement was digested by the ladies. Mrs. Potts adjusted her hat smugly.

"I'm sure her memory does not go back that far, Mrs. Potts," said Mrs. Lawson. "Since she must be close to your age," she added hurriedly, not understanding why she would want to appease Mrs. Potts in any possible way, but not being able to stop herself.

"Yes, I suppose," said a slightly mollified Mrs. Potts. "But memory's a funny thing. What starts as fantasy can turn to fact over the years, don't you agree?" She snapped her mouth shut in sudden silence when she saw Marilla Cuthbert enter the hall with Rachel Lynde.

Marilla was painfully aware of the sudden halt in conversation on her entrance. She wished fervently that she had followed her own best instincts and not allowed Rachel to talk her into attending the rummage sale. She had known full well that news of her little "romance" would have spread far and wide. She was not so naive as to think otherwise. However, she had hoped against hope that once the subject of Duncan McTavish had been thoroughly discussed, it would be dismissed as yesterday's news. She realized now, as she looked at the bemused faces surrounding her, all trying their best to pretend that they were not looking at her, that such would never be the case in Avonlea. They might chew upon the subject and bury it for a while, but, like dogs with an old bone, they would dig it up and chew upon it again and again, with renewed vigor.

Marilla looked towards Mrs. Potts and the group of ladies near the jam and preserves table, straightened her shoulders and gave them a small, dignified nod of greeting.

The ladies all smiled their brightest social smiles and then turned to each other with pursed lips. Marilla looked skyward.

Rachel, a basket of red-currant preserves over her arm, had eyes only for the tea table. To her chagrin, Hetty King was serving, acting for all the world as if she were in charge, when in fact she, Rachel, had done most of the organizational work.

"Wouldn't you know that she'd be presiding over the tea table." Rachel shook her head in annoyance. "I wouldn't sit down to tea with Hetty King if it were the last cup on earth."

Marilla looked at Rachel wearily. "Rachel, don't you think it's about time you buried that old hatchet?"

"Ha!" snorted Rachel. "When I bury that hatchet, I'll be under the ground next to it."

Marilla shook her head imperceptibly and headed towards the tea table, quite unaware of the events that were about to unfold.

Chapter Twelve

Sara raced down the road towards the Town Hall, holding her hat with one hand lest it fly off her head completely. She was not giving one thought to the consequences of arriving at the rummage sale without the fateful handkerchief. She had far more exciting things on her mind than that. Visions of Marilla Cuthbert's face wreathed in smiles of joy and relief filled her imagination. Reunited with her beau after so many years of uncertainty and longing. What tidings to be able to deliver!

As she approached the white clapboard building, Sara could see there was still a crowd of people lined up outside the Town Hall, all waiting for their chance to go in. Sara had no intention of waiting. She wove in and out of the crowd, mumbling "Excuse me" and "Pardon me" and all the things she knew she ought to say. She said an extra sincere "I'm sorry" to a woman whose foot unfortunately found its way under her shoe. Sara burst through the front door of the hall, scanning the crowd for the one person she sought, the one and only person who should be the recipient of her news. She spotted Marilla coaxing Rachel towards the tea table.

"Miss Cuthbert!" called Sara.

Rachel immediately spun around and fixed her eyes on the flushed, excited Sara. All heads in the room swiveled to where Sara stood in the doorway. Marilla turned slowly, embarrassed to have so much attention called to herself in the middle of such a crowd.

"For pity's sake, child! What is it?"

Sara approached Marilla through the crowd. She whispered excitedly, "Miss Cuthbert! He's here!"

For the life of her, Marilla could not make out what Sara was saying. "Pardon me?" she said, peering at Sara over the top of her glasses.

Perhaps Marilla was hard of hearing, considered Sara. She'd had enough sense to realize what the reaction of the women in the crowd would be to her news, and she didn't want to say it much louder than she already had, so she repeated herself with clearer pronunciation.

"He's here! In Avonlea!"

"Who?" asked an exasperated Marilla, not seeing at all what the child was getting at.

"*He* is!" enunciated Sara as clearly as she could, equally exasperated.

By this time, Rachel was more anxious than Marilla to understand what Sara was trying to say.

"Who is 'he'?" she and Marilla asked Sara in the same breath. Marilla turned and gave Rachel a look that would wither buds on a vine.

Sara could contain herself no longer. "Duncan McTavish! He's here in Avonlea!" she burst out, in a much louder voice than she had intended.

The effect of her announcement was instantaneous.

Marilla Cuthbert went quite pale and sat down upon the nearest chair.

Every single person in the hall—man, woman and child—turned to stare at Sara and Marilla.

"He's here?" exclaimed an astonished Mrs. Biggins.

"Did she say Duncan McTavish?" Olivia whispered to Hetty at the tea table.

"He's in Avonlea?" said a delighted Felicity, heading towards Sara, with such excitement that she even neglected to accept the money that was being handed to her for one of her serving napkins.

For once in her life, Mrs. Potts was too taken aback to utter even a word.

From all corners of the hall, people descended on Marilla and Sara.

"How do you know it's him?" demanded Mrs. Biggins.

"His name is right on his sign," replied an excited Sara.

"What sign?" asked Sally Potts, impudently sidling over with her mother, annoyed that Sara should be such a center of attention.

"In front of the general store. He has a stand! And his first name is Duncan!"

"Where is he from?" Mrs. Potts asked, positive that she alone could prove Sara's story wrong and nip this whole extraordinary scene in the bud.

"New Brunswick, but he's living out West now!"

Mrs. Potts's mouth fell open.

Sara looked at Marilla, fully expecting the imagined wreath of smiles. Marilla remained pale and still.

"What does he look like?" Felicity demanded.

"He's oh, so comely! And he told Mr. Lawson he was a bachelor, so you see, he has never forgotten you, Marilla!"

Sara could barely control her excitement, but she was beginning to have doubts about her own imaginative abilities. Marilla Cuthbert was certainly not reacting at all as she had pictured she might. The lady in fact remained as still and silent as if she were in some sort of a trance. All eyes looked upon her with great anticipation. Marilla realized that she must say something, do something. She put down her teacup and broke the expectant silence. "It's impossible," she said faintly. "It can't be the...same Duncan McTavish."

"Well, how do you know it isn't?" Rachel's

sharp voice cut through the silence like a knife.

Marilla took a deep breath and looked over her shoulder at Rachel. "Take my word for it, Rachel. It can't be," she said wryly.

"But it could be." As usual, Rachel was not to be put off easily.

Mrs. Lawson and her niece, with the kindest intentions, bent down to speak to Marilla. "You have to meet with him, Marilla! Just to make sure!" said Mrs. Lawson.

"If it were me, I'd simply die of curiosity," added her niece.

Marilla remained silent. The crowd of course thought this a most appropriate reaction to such news. Marilla was obviously in shock, and rightly so. Sara looked from Marilla to the group of women around her, and wondered if she could have announced her news any differently to have had the effect that she had hoped for. Grown-ups were so odd at times. Marilla was clearly not pleased. Quite the opposite, in fact.

"You do want to see him, don't you?" asked Sara timidly.

"Well, Marilla?" prompted Mrs. Potts nastily, still of the belief that there was something fishy about the whole affair, whether the man was from New Brunswick or not.

Marilla pulled herself together with a dignity

that never failed her, even in the most awkward moments. "Even if it were the same Duncan McTavish, why would I want to see him? That book has been put on the shelf and I don't intend to open it again," she said slowly and decisively.

Once again, Rachel was not to be put off. She huffed in disagreement. "Oh fiddlesticks, Marilla. There wouldn't be any harm in it."

Marilla took a deep breath. "I have always believed in letting bygones be bygones." She rose from her chair and pulled herself to her full height. "Now, let's not say anything more about it." Her tone of voice made it clear that that was to be the last word spoken on the subject.

The ladies were silenced, and Marilla hoped against hope that they would respect her wish. Inevitably, however, Rachel could not help but urge her friend to consider another point of view—her own.

"Seems to me, Marilla, you're making a mountain out of a mole-hill. It would be the most natural thing in the world for you to stop by and give him your regards, even if he is a Methodist."

Marilla turned and looked daggers at Rachel.

"Rachel, what I choose to do in this situation is my business! Not yours or anyone else's in

Avonlea! And I would thank you to keep your snooping, interfering nose out of it!"

Rachel was by turns surprised, humiliated and furious at this public outburst, and in characteristic form, she turned the accusation right back on Marilla.

"Marilla, are you hiding something?"

"Nothing but my temper, Rachel," said Marilla tersely.

Rachel Lynde held on tenaciously. "It's my belief there's more to this than you're telling us, Marilla. Makes me wonder if you aren't leading us all down the garden path?"

Marilla tried very hard to retain her composure. "I beg your pardon?" she asked Rachel quietly.

Rachel instantly realized that she had gone just one tiny step too far. She planted a conciliatory smile upon her face.

"Well, you needn't be so indignant Marilla. The less fuss the better, in my opinion. We all make mistakes. Just put it behind you."

This was the last straw for Marilla. Rachel's attempt at forgiving and forgetting had had the opposite effect.

"Rachel Lynde, if you are insinuating what I think you are, your so-called friendship means less to me than...than...a jar of your red-currant preserves!"

Marilla slammed her teacup down into its

saucer, spilling nearly all its contents, and swept out of the hall, the crowd of men and women parting like waves before her.

"Well, I see I have to be very careful of what I say around you, Marilla!" called Rachel after her, before stomping off in the opposite direction.

The women stared. "Marilla Cuthbert won't be paler than that in her coffin," Hetty King was heard to comment.

"It must be such a shock to her." Olivia shook her head in sympathy.

"In more ways than one," said Mrs. Potts, her tone ripe with sarcasm.

"I thought she would be happy," said a mystified Sara, looking down at her feet in true disappointment. She had never in the world meant to upset Marilla Cuthbert, and now it seemed that she had done exactly that. She would have to make things right, one way or another.

Chapter Thirteen

"Step right up folks!" called Duncan McTavish. "You will be amazed at the powers of this treatment. McTavish Porous Plasters cure croup, bronchitis and many other congestive symptoms overnight. It comes highly recommended by respected doctors across Canada. I have a collection of their statements for anyone interested."

A large group of people gathered around Duncan McTavish's buggy in front of Lawson's general store. The man himself, in his three-piece suit with a gold watch chain across his chest, smiled confidently in the knowledge that where there is a crowd, there is business. He greeted the townsfolk and shook hands like a seasoned politician. He liberally handed out printed sheets of testimony to all who reached for them, and continued his pitch.

"I have already received favorable comments from customers who have bought my product since I've been here."

Mr. and Mrs. Lawson watched from the steps of the general store. Mr. Lawson shook his head in disbelief. "Doesn't that beat all? I haven't seen crowds like that since Melville Sloane held cockfights on Friday nights. Mind you," he added, "I've been watching, and they're doing a lot of looking and listening, but they're not buying his product. I did advise him that that would probably be the case."

Mrs. Lawson nodded wisely. "I don't think it's Duncan McTavish's Porous Plasters that are attracting these people, my dear!"

Mr. McTavish scanned the crowd of curious

onlookers, knowing that nothing sells better than live testimony.

"Mrs. Ira Biggins, would you please step right up here and tell the folks about the wonderful result you had from McTavish's Porous Plasters?" Duncan McTavish motioned to a bashful Mrs. Biggins, who came out of the crowd, smiling coyly at him from under the brim of her straw hat. She accepted his hand as he assisted her gallantly to the podium.

"My, are all the gentlemen from Blakely, New Brunswick as strong as you, Mr. McTavish?" She took care to emphasize the word "Blakely."

Mr. McTavish looked truly puzzled. "I beg your pardon?" he asked the smiling Mrs. Biggins.

"Well, that is where you're from, isn't it?" she asked inquisitively, aware of the many ears around her trying to catch the answer of the gentleman in question.

Duncan McTavish smiled back, determined to humor the woman, for, in spite of the fact that she seemed slightly dotty, she was his only live testimonial, and he was determined to make the most of her.

"Well then, Mrs. Biggins." He cleared his throat. "Please impart what you told to me about McTavish's Porous Plasters to the rest of these gracious people."

Mrs. Biggins looked disappointed at not receiving the answer she had hoped for, but, to her credit, she did hold forth on the subject of porous plasters.

"My husband Ira had complained of a strained shoulder muscle just last night, having loaded the hay in the barn the day before."

Mrs. Biggins stopped and smiled again at Mr. McTavish, trying to picture him and Marilla Cuthbert as young lovers. This was very difficult for her, however, as her imaginative powers were fairly limited.

"Go on, Mrs. Biggins. What did you decide to do?" coaxed Mr. McTavish.

"Oh! Well, I had the sample you gave me, Mr. McTavish, and so I applied a plaster, and lo and behold—"

"What sort of plaster, Mrs. Biggins?" prompted Mr. McTavish.

"McTavish's Porous Plaster, of course," replied a smiling Mrs. Biggins on cue.

"And how was your husband feeling this morning, my dear madam?"

"He was right as rain this morning. That's a fact!"

"Thank you, Mrs. Biggins!" said a grateful Mr. McTavish, extending his hand and helping her down from the podium.

A mumble from the crowd gave him reason to believe that a number of sales would inevitably follow. However, as Mrs. Lawson had predicted, most of the conversations did not center on the subject of porous plasters.

"Rachel Lynde told me that Marilla Cuthbert has not set foot out of Green Gables since the rummage sale," said one lady in the crowd to another.

"Well naturally," replied her friend. "Marilla can't risk coming face to face with him. It's plain as plain can be that he's never laid eyes on her before in his life."

"It's my opinion that Marilla is guilty of a falsehood and that's the plain, ugly truth," said Mrs. Potts, to anyone who cared to listen.

Mrs. Charlotte Maxwell, a fine, upstanding dowager of advanced years, looked scornfully at Mrs. Potts from under the veil of her proper, navy-blue hat, as though Mrs. Potts had just committed a great sin indeed.

"Fiddlesticks. There isn't a more honest soul in Avonlea than Marilla Cuthbert." She walked away from Mrs. Potts in a huff, her shoulders stiff with rebuke.

Unaware of the controversy, Mr. McTavish took Mrs. Biggins's place on the podium. "Step right up, folks!" he repeated, maintaining his smile and his general good humor. "Help me pay my rent tonight!"

People mumbled to each other and then set off on their daily errands. Mr. McTavish looked at the dispersing crowds with concern.

From their vantage point on the steps of the general store, Mr. and Mrs. Lawson watched as people went on their way.

"Well, I don't know what to think," said a thoughtful Mrs. Lawson, shaking her head. "But I'd certainly like to be a fly on the wall at Green Gables!"

Chapter Fourteen

Indeed, the flies in the kitchen at Green Gables were very likely the only inhabitants of that dwelling blissfully buzzing about, without a care in the world.

Always a fearfully conscientious housekeeper, Marilla had outdone herself over the past week. The floors, walls and every surface of the kitchen had been scoured, and they gleamed with a high polish, a result of an obsessive bout of feverish cleaning.

A very grim-faced Marilla was now in the process of preparing dinner. She paced back and forth between table and stove, china cabinet and table, with the air of someone carrying a great weight on her back. She set the table with two place settings. She stalked back to the stove and stirred the stew with a vengeance, taking out whatever conflicts stirred within her on its contents. She reached for the pot lid from where it lay on the stove top, and just as her fingers touched its burning metal she let go of it with a clatter, exclaiming in pain. The lid rolled along the floor and, with a repetitive rattle, finally came to rest.

Outside in the hall, Rachel jumped when she heard the clatter and then peeked cautiously through a crack in the door.

Marilla instantly felt a tingling in the middle of her backbone, the unmistakable feeling that usually accompanies being watched. She turned swiftly and caught a glimpse of Rachel's nose, just as the door to the kitchen quietly shut.

Rachel paced fretfully, not sure whether to enter the kitchen or not.

Marilla breathed deeply and held her burnt fingers under the cold running water of the pump. She threw a baleful look towards the door.

"Rachel, you have to eat. Stop skulking in the hall."

A long-faced Rachel appeared in the doorway.

She inched her way into the room slowly, eyeing Marilla cautiously.

"If you'd rather I took supper in my room, Marilla, just say so. I'd prefer that to silence."

"Do as you like, Rachel," said Marilla shortly, drying her aching hand on a towel, still not meeting Rachel's eyes.

Rachel watched her with mounting exasperation. It was hard for her to keep things bottled up, and for the last few days she had thought she would burst if she didn't speak her mind.

"Well, if you ask me, Marilla, you're not yourself!" she began, no longer able to hold her tongue. "Hiding away in this house. Even Reverend Leonard noticed your absence from church on Sunday, and he wouldn't notice a fly on the end of his nose. I don't know why you bother to cook! You barely touch your food! Now, I'm not one to meddle, but—"

Marilla cut her off with another great clatter of pots and pan lids. "Ha!" She exclaimed. "Not one to meddle? Rachel! You must be dreaming!"

"I don't call speaking the truth meddling!" retorted Rachel.

Marilla seized the ladle and threw stew onto a plate, then slapped it down on the table in front of the indignant Rachel.

"This supposed gentleman friend of yours is

right here, in Avonlea!" said Rachel slowly, with emphasis. "You can't stay away from him entirely, unless, of course, as everyone is saying, you didn't know him in the first place."

Marilla stopped in her tracks. For days she had been torn, as she had never been before in her life, between confession and pride. Rachel's insinuations, however, were more than she could bear, and pride won out.

"Rachel Lynde, I took you in after Thomas died because you didn't want to go out West and live with your children!" Her voice shook with emotion. "Talk about taking a viper to your bosom!"

Marilla stormed out the kitchen door onto the porch, slamming the screen behind her.

"You're stubborn, Marilla! Stubborn and proud! That's what!" Rachel shouted after her, still unwilling to let Marilla have the last word.

Marilla said nothing, and Rachel watched her as she strode down the lawn toward the vegetable garden.

Chapter Fifteen

Compared to the goings on at Green Gables, the porch at Rose Cottage was a picture of tranquility. The wild roses entwined themselves around the lattice and the freshly painted white arbors, the pinks and peaches of their petals almost iridescent in the rays of the setting sun.

On the steps, Sara sat shelling peas. On one side of her sat her Aunt Olivia, concentrating on some exquisite needlework. On her other side, Aunt Hetty sat peeling apples.

Sara was quite content to shell peas. It was the type of work that didn't require one's total attention, and therefore it allowed her imagination to run as freely as she wished. At this moment her thoughts were filled with the dilemma of Marilla Cuthbert and her thwarted love. In a strange way, Sara felt vaguely responsible for all that had happened, and even though her Aunt Hetty had assured her that all would unfold in this world as it should, somehow this was not an adequate way for Sara to leave things.

"But if Miss Cuthbert doesn't talk to Mr. McTavish," she persisted, "he will think she still cherishes bitterness against him, and there will be no chance of a reconciliation. Their quarrel will never be made up. I wish there was something I could do."

Olivia looked at Sara, her huge brown eyes filled with a sadness far beyond Marilla's present predicament.

"Sara, affairs of the heart need time to unfold on their own. Interference never helps." Olivia flashed a meaningful look at her older sister.

Hetty caught Olivia's glance but deliberately ignored it, addressing her next remark to Sara alone.

"Sometimes interference is necessary," she said pointedly. "Most people in that situation are not in their right minds. They can't think straight."

"My mind was completely clear about Edwin Clarke, Hetty. You should never have interfered between him and me. You drove him away!" burst out Olivia, obviously distressed.

"Aha!" declared Hetty. "So you were willing to go traipsing all over the world with that shiftless dreamer?"

Olivia took a deep breath and turned a much brighter shade of pink than the roses that curled around the trellis behind her. Hetty turned away from her.

Sara looked from one aunt to the other. Edwin Clarke, she thought to herself—the beau Olivia mentioned at the sewing circle and everyone else seemed to know about. So, for once Mrs. Potts could be taken at her word. Her Aunt Hetty really had intervened. Poor Aunt Olivia. Who would have thought that such sadness lurked beneath her sunny exterior? Sara was again filled with the wonder of the secrets that grown-ups were able to conceal. She shuddered to think that both her beautiful aunt and Marilla Cuthbert could possibly suffer the rest of their lives from unrequited love.

Aunt Hetty interrupted her thoughts. "Believe me, Sara, if I hadn't intervened, your Aunt Olivia would probably be next to your mother in the churchyard, six feet under!" She said tersely, giving the handle of the apple-peeler a vicious crank.

"Hetty, don't fill the child's head with such nonsense!" Olivia turned to Sara and said in a much gentler tone, "Sara, some things have to be left to Providence."

Hetty snorted. "There are times, Sara, when Providence needs a little human intervention."

Olivia sighed but decided to keep her own counsel. When Hetty was in this sort of a mood, there was no point in pressing a point further, however valid it was.

Sara concentrated on shelling peas as a thick silence descended on either side of her. She felt quite helpless. If only she had been around when Edwin Clarke had come courting, things might have worked out differently, in spite of Aunt Hetty or Providence. She realized that there was nothing she could do to help poor

Aunt Olivia now, but she could still do her best where Marilla Cuthbert and Duncan McTavish were concerned. What was it Aunt Hetty had said? "Sometimes Providence needs a little human intervention." It was obvious that Marilla Cuthbert and Duncan McTavish were both simply too stubborn to ever let Providence make much of a difference in the course of their lives, and if what her Aunt Hetty had said were true, then it was up to someone to intervene on their behalf.

In the kitchen later that evening, Sara was still puzzling about what course of action she should take as she helped dry the dinner dishes and put them away. Her Aunt Olivia had excused herself early, still quiet and withdrawn after her discussion with her sister earlier that evening.

Hetty blew out one of the lamps as Sara replaced the very last glass on the shelf.

"Thank you, Sara. Well now, off to bed with you," said her aunt, as she moved briskly around the room.

Sara watched her, unable to decide whether to ask her advice or not. She finally concluded that it certainly would do no harm, especially if she posed the question very carefully.

"Aunt Hetty?"

Hetty turned from the counter, surprised to

see Sara still standing in the shadows of the kitchen. "Yes Sara?" she asked.

"You know when you said those things about human intervention...?" began Sara, leaning against the table, fiddling with a napkin that lay there.

Hetty had to think for a moment. "Yes?" She picked up the napkin and put it away in its proper place.

Sara took a deep breath. "Well, if you had a friend...actually, not really a friend...but someone you had met, and you thought that they might be...slightly frightened about a situation...and you knew that there was something that you could do, not really to help them, but to...cause something to happen...that the lady...that the friend, wouldn't do themselves, do you think it's best to do what your heart says or let Divine Providence help out instead?"

Hetty stared at Sara, hoping that the dim light of the kitchen would prevent the child from seeing how utterly perplexed she was. She groped for an answer that wouldn't betray how completely she had missed the point of the question, if it, in fact, had been a question, and if, in fact, there had been a point. She was most aware that she must not, at all costs, appear to be ill-equipped to answer the question of a child. She was a teacher, after all, was she not?

"Sara," she began slowly, her face taking on a look of unfathomable wisdom, "Providence isn't just there to help us out of every little difficulty. Providence helps those who help themselves." She paused. "Does that...uh...answer your question?"

Sara responded by flying across the room and giving her aunt a bear hug. Unaccustomed as she was to impulsive displays of affection, Hetty tentatively hugged back, smiling in spite of herself. Then she delicately disentangled herself from Sara's embrace.

"You must always come to me with your problems, Sara," she said gravely.

Sara's face beamed at her in the darkened kitchen. "I will. Thank you, Aunt Hetty. Goodnight!"

Sara left her maiden aunt standing in the middle of her kitchen with a look of almost motherly pride on her face. But slowly, her self-satisfaction turned to puzzlement. Whatever did the child mean?

Chapter Sixteen

The first faint light of morning touched the eastern sky, and the mist rose from the fields and forests that surrounded the village of Avonlea.

The winding road to Rose Cottage turned from dark ochre to warm red as the sun's rays dried the dew and dappled it with the shadows of the drooping, sleepy leaves.

Lace curtains fluttered in the breeze, throwing sunny patches of light on the cabbage roses that papered the walls of Sara's room. Suddenly, the quilts were thrown back and Sara sat bolt upright. For a dreadful moment she thought she had over-slept, and she leapt out of bed and ran across the surprisingly cold floor to her window. She was greatly comforted to see the sun still so close to the horizon. It was time to put her plan into play.

The night before, she had carefully laid out her clothes so that it would take no time at all to dress. She threw off her nightgown and literally jumped into her bloomers and petticoats. Her dress went over her head and she struggled with its tiny buttons that went up the back, right to the top of the high neck. Usually, Aunt Olivia helped her with them. She was at the door with her hand on the knob when she realized she had not put her stockings and shoes on. She struggled with the wretched stockings and pulled on her shoes. Why did laces always take so long to do up when one was in a hurry, she wondered to herself as she impatiently pulled them tight.

If Hetty King had not been slumbering in her

bed, comfortable in her eiderdown and her dreams, she might have seen a figure sneak stealthily out of a bedroom, down the stairs and out the front door.

Outside, Sara breathed deeply the sweet morning air. The roses were crystallized with dew. They looked exactly like the sugar roses Sara remembered on birthday cakes from so long ago. Something magical was bound to happen on a day such as this one. She let herself quietly out the garden gate and ran off in the direction of town.

No one yet stirred in Avonlea in the early hours of morning. Mabel Sloane hadn't yet opened the post office. Mr. Lawson had not arrived to put out his barrels of apples and baskets of potatoes. Sara shivered, and not just from the chill of the air. Avonlea was almost like a ghost town in the early morning mist.

She made her way down the silent street toward the "McTavish Porous Plaster" buggy, still closed and locked for the night in front of the general store. A horse neighed gently from the direction of the blacksmith's shop as she approached it. She stopped and stood in its shadow, not knowing quite what she would do if Mr. McTavish were not to appear.

She needn't have worried. The sound of whistling came from the direction of Mrs. Biggins's boarding house. Sara slipped behind the buggy out of sight and peeked around to see Mr. Duncan McTavish strolling down the boarding house path and out the gate. He walked with a jaunty stride, straightening the straw boater on his head. Sara pulled back as he got closer.

As soon as Mr. McTavish reached his buggy, he took a large key from his pocket and unlocked it, unfolding its sides to show his advertisements to their full advantage. Very quietly, Sara came out of hiding.

"Excuse me, Mr. McTavish?"

The gentleman jumped in surprise and whirled around, totally unaware that anyone was about. He stared into the huge, serious blue eyes that faced him. "My goodness, child. You gave me a scare. What can I do for you so early this fine morning?"

Sara tried to form her words in her mind before she said them. Quite often, grown-ups were not inclined to take children seriously, especially a strange child that they had never laid eyes on before. She took a deep breath. "Mr. McTavish, my name is Sara Stanley, and I've come to talk to you about a most important matter of the heart," she said in an extremely grave voice. "It concerns a lady by the name of Marilla Cuthbert."

"Marilla Cuthbert?" Mr. McTavish frowned

slightly, his face showing nothing but confusion. "Never heard of her."

"Oh, grief is the saddest thing," said Sara. "You can't have completely blocked her name from your memory. The key must still be there to unlock that secret door in your heart!"

Mr. McTavish looked quite bewildered as he tried his utmost to understand what this strange little girl was endeavoring to communicate to him.

"What on heaven's earth are you talking about, young lady?"

Sara swallowed hard. How could he behave this way? Perhaps Methodists were quite different after all. Most certainly, he was as stubborn as Miss Cuthbert had intimated he was.

"I would never have come here to talk to you like this, sir, but for the fact that she is full of pride and refuses to face you."

Duncan McTavish continued to look completely at sea.

Sara persisted. "You must forgive her. You cannot treat a lady of the calibre of Marilla Cuthbert in such a fashion. Please go and see her before you leave Avonlea. I beg you."

"And I beg you, young lady, to tell me what this is all about!" replied Mr. McTavish, becoming increasingly disturbed.

As the fates would have it, who should have

sidled by along the street at that very moment but the early-rising Mrs. Potts. She was never one to miss much, and the moment she spotted Sara in conversation with Mr. McTavish, she, of course, ambled closer to listen, looking very interested indeed.

Sara was beginning to think that perhaps Mr. McTavish had suffered a dreadful memory loss. Her Aunt Hetty had told her that some people were prone to this as they grew older. But surely Mr. McTavish was not of such an advanced age as to be stricken with such a handicap. She felt she must jog his memory in any case.

"But Miss Cuthbert told me all about you," she began. "You were her beau. You met her in Blakely, New Brunswick, many years ago. Don't you remember?"

"Young lady, I don't know what you're talking about!" The gentleman was beginning to be considerably annoyed and went back to setting up his buggy for the day's business. Mrs. Potts seized her opportunity and sauntered over to them.

"Excuse me, I couldn't help overhearing," said the lady in her sweetest voice.

Sara looked at her in horror, fully realizing how dangerous the situation could be if Mrs. Potts were to become involved.

"Do you mean to say you are not from Blakely," Mrs. Potts asked slowly, savoring every word that might lead to the proof she so needed to confirm her doubts about Marilla's story.

"No! Saint John," said Mr. McTavish firmly. Sara's eyes widened.

"Now isn't that interesting," said Mrs. Potts, with the charm of a snake. "That's not what Marilla Cuthbert said."

"Who is this Marilla Cuthbert? Would someone please tell me what this is all about?" Duncan McTavish was starting to get quite angry. Sara stood rooted to the spot in fear as his voice rose. She watched as the skin above his tight, starched collar reddened and his eyes flashed.

"I'm not one to spread idle gossip, Mr. McTavish." Sara winced as Mrs. Potts spoke with a voice as smooth as silk. "But I'm surprised the story hasn't already reached your ears. The town has been talking about it since the day you arrived."

By now Mr. McTavish's entire face was crimson, and he spoke with a barely controlled, quiet voice.

"I have no idea what they would have to talk about! I don't know a soul in this town! But I do know that I'm not going to allow my name to be slandered, once again! The old gossips in the last one-horse town I was in had me in cahoots with the minister's wife! Once that untruth spread, my stand was empty! No business!"

He stopped and took a breath. Mrs. Potts opened her mouth to interject, but he cut her off before she had a chance to utter a syllable.

"What is wrong with you people? Is there so little going on in your own little lives that you have to fall on a stranger and assassinate his character?"

Mrs. Potts backed off slightly, not quite prepared for this confrontation, her mouth pursed with concern. Sara started to shrink away as well. Mr. McTavish's tirade had not finished, however.

"Well this time I'm not going to stand by and have my name dragged through the mud by another small-town, small-minded old biddy! Where does this woman live?"

He bent down and glared at Sara, waiting for an answer, his angry face inches from her own. Sara was horrified and took off at a run down the street.

"Come back here!" yelled Mr. McTavish after her. "Where does she live?"

Sara did not even turn around. Once again, Mrs. Potts saw an opportunity that she just could not waste. "I'll be glad to tell you where Marilla

Cuthbert lives," she said, with a voice that dripped honey.

Mr. McTavish took a deep breath and attempted to quell his anger. "Thank you, madam," he said, tipping his hat. "I would simply like to nip this little situation in the bud."

"Believe me, so would I, Mr. McTavish. So would I," said Mrs. Potts.

Sara had already reached the outskirts of Avonlea and raced across a field that would take her to Green Gables. She hoped and prayed that she would not be too late.

Chapter Seventeen

The kitchen at Green Gables was thick with steam. Marilla Cuthbert was boiling clothes in a huge pot on top of the stove. She stirred the heavy garments with a stick, her face bright with perspiration, her hair straying from the prison of the tight bun atop her head. She leaned wearily against the stick and wiped her face with the back of her hand.

The last week or so had not been kind to Marilla. She had still not opened her mouth to speak a word to Rachel. She had still not been to the village since the day of the rummage sale.

Instead, she had chosen to shut herself away like a hermit, totally aware of what would happen if she came face to face with this Duncan McTavish fellow. She knew that she could not continue this behavior forever, but she was holding on for dear life to the fact that the man was a traveling salesman, and therefore, at some point in the near future he would surely travel onward. She prayed for that moment to arrive.

She was tormented beyond belief, her normal good sense crying out for her to set things right. But no one had ever disputed the fact that Marilla Cuthbert was stubborn.

She was in the middle of turning all of these thoughts over in her mind for the one-hundredth time that morning when there was a clatter of running feet on the porch. The clatter was followed by a loud knocking on the door.

Marilla wiped her hands on her apron and slowly made her way to the door. The knocking grew louder and more insistent. Marilla opened the door, and facing her across the threshold was an out-of-breath Sara Stanley, obviously very disturbed and upset.

"Mercy, child! What do you want?" said Marilla, letting her in.

Sara was teary and breathless, and the words tumbled out of her mouth. "I'm sorry to disturb you, Miss Cuthbert, but I must speak to you. I've just done the most awful thing! I didn't mean it to be, but..."

Marilla led her to a kitchen chair and sat her down upon it. "Calm yourself. Now, what in Heaven's name have you done?"

Sara looked at Marilla, her eyes imploring the lady to understand. "I thought I was helping. I went to Duncan McTavish and told him...your story. And, and..." Sara didn't quite know how to say it.

"Yes...?" Marilla urged her on.

"Oh Miss Cuthbert," Sara blurted out. "He didn't seem to know who you were at all!"

Marilla sat herself down on one of the kitchen chairs. Her chest rose and fell as she took several deep breaths. "If there is one thing in this life that we can be perfectly sure of, it's that if you do wrong, you'll be punished for it sometime, somehow or somewhere," she murmured, almost to herself. She looked up at Sara, who was watching her closely with mournful eyes. "Well, child, what did he say?" she asked, resigned to know the worst.

"Miss Cuthbert, he acted as if he had never heard of you in his entire life. But I think what's worse is what Mrs. Potts is going to say." Sara's voice trailed off.

"Mrs. Potts was there?" asked the poor woman in a sharp voice.

Sara nodded slowly.

"Oh good Lord!" said Marilla, rubbing a hand over her eyes. She took another deep breath, and her features softened slightly as she looked at Sara's intensely honest face. "Sara, I am more of an old, foolish woman than you know."

The kitchen door to the hall opened suddenly, and Rachel Lynde stuck her nose in. "Marilla, there is a gentleman here to see you!" she hissed.

Marilla took a sharp breath. "What sort of gentleman, Rachel?"

"It's none but Duncan McTavish, that's what! And he's mad as a hornet." Rachel turned and looked over her shoulder, as if expecting the man would pounce on her the moment her back was to him. She centered her attention on the kitchen once again, awaiting Marilla's reply.

Marilla stood up and straightened her shoulders. "Show him to the sitting room, Rachel, and tell him I'll be there directly," she said quietly.

Marilla shared a look with Sara, but, resigned to her fate, she rolled down her sleeves and straightened her collar. She then walked stiffly and calmly to the door, with the air of a person being led to the gallows.

"Oh Miss Cuthbert, I'm so sorry! It's all my fault!" called Sara after her, almost in tears.

Marilla turned and looked at Sara, her eyes full of the memories of another little girl who had brought both trouble and warmth to her household so many years ago. She shook her head. "Little girls..." she said wryly, and left the room.

Chapter Eighteen

The heavy velvet curtains were drawn in the sitting room at Green Gables, and for a moment after she had quietly entered the room, Marilla could not make out if anyone was there at all. A movement near one of the windows, however, made her heart lurch in a most disconcerting way. Knowing that Rachel would be apt to eavesdrop, she closed the door firmly behind her.

Rachel, who in fact was hovering in the hallway just outside the room, with Sara close behind her, jumped back just in time to prevent certain injury to her nose.

Marilla stood as firmly as she was able, her hand still on the doorknob to steady her, her heart beating wildly.

A tall figure emerged from the shadows and stepped forward into a patch of sunlight. His face was red with anger and impatience. He took off his hat and turned it with agitation.

"Miss Cuthbert?" he inquired gruffly.

"Yes," said Marilla, barely finding her voice.

"Need I introduce myself?" inquired the gentleman.

On the other side of the sitting room door, an astonished Rachel gasped in surprise at his remark. Did he mean that he didn't need introducing? Was it possible that Marilla had previously made this gentleman's acquaintance after all?

Sara watched Mrs. Lynde with interest. It was obvious that the lady did not know the truth about Marilla Cuthbert and Duncan McTavish. Sara wasn't sure whether or not she knew it either. Miss Cuthbert certainly had not seemed overly surprised that the man had no recollection of her. On the other hand, he had greeted her as if he knew her.

Marilla glanced once again toward the door, fully aware that Rachel was most likely listening on the other side of it. She would have to contrive to get Duncan McTavish out of hearing range as quickly as she could.

"Could we go into the garden?" she began, with some hesitation in her voice. "It is much less stuffy there."

"I...suppose so. Yes," said Mr. McTavish grumpily. His manner, however, had become somewhat less gruff at the sight of Marilla. Her face was flushed and in the pale, early morning sunlight of the room she looked ten years younger. He couldn't help but be struck by an honesty and intelligence on the lady's face that he had not expected.

Marilla led the way through the door to the garden, Duncan McTavish following her. The moment they left the room, the door opened slowly and cautiously, and Rachel Lynde tiptoed in and to the window, in search of a vantage point. She stationed herself behind the heavy curtains of a window facing out to the garden. Sara joined her.

Chapter Nineteen

Marilla led Mr. McTavish out onto the lawn. The fresh air and the serenity of the garden helped her to compose herself somewhat, and she stood quietly, full of guilt, waiting for the outpouring of wrath that was bound to manifest itself.

A curtain twitched in the sitting room window as Rachel placed herself in a spot from which she could see all.

Mr. McTavish turned to Marilla, trying to maintain his fury, determined to say all the things he had rehearsed in his mind since Mrs. Potts had directed him to this house.

"Now look here, Miss Cuthbert," he began sternly. "Apparently, some tale is circulating all over Avonlea, and I aim to get to the bottom of it!"

Marilla held her chin up and nodded stiffly for him to continue.

Mr. McTavish took a deep breath. "I'd like to know what on God's Earth gave you the right to tell people we were...involved in some way?"

Two spots of color rose on Marilla's cheeks, and she looked down at her feet, but said nothing.

"Do you know what it has done to my business?" he went on, his voice rising. "I wondered at the large crowds and no sales! Now I see I was just an object of curiosity for all the tongue-wagging old..."

Marilla glanced up at him in agony, her face openly displaying her own misery at all he was saying to her. Mr. McTavish looked at Marilla, his sails instantly deflating. He interpreted her open anguish of guilt as innocence and immediately started to regret his initial anger.

"I feel quite foolish..." he began slowly. "Because, just by looking at you, I can tell you are not the type of person to make up stories. I have been a victim of gossip once again. Just excuse me and I'll go away and kick myself."

From the folds of the curtain, Rachel watched with interest as Mr. McTavish turned to go. Sara breathed a sigh of relief.

Marilla watched as well as Mr. McTavish tipped his hat to her and made his way across the lawn. "No!" she called, finding her voice. Mr. McTavish turned and looked at her with inquiring eyes. "No. Please," murmured Marilla, swallowing. "You mustn't go until you have learned the truth."

Mr. McTavish looked very puzzled, as well he might, but he turned and walked slowly back to where Marilla stood.

From a perplexed Rachel Lynde's point of view behind the curtains, it looked just like a lover's quarrel that now seemed to be on the mend. The man had clearly been leaving in a huff not two moments ago. And yet here he was, rejoining Marilla with a supercilious look on his face. She threw a flabbergasted look in Sara's direction.

"Well doesn't that beat all! Trust a Methodist to change his mind!"

Mr. McTavish waited patiently for Marilla to speak.

"I have a confession to make," said Marilla slowly. "I...I did tell those stories."

Mr. McTavish frowned and opened his mouth to speak, thought better of it and closed it again.

Marilla continued. "But, you must believe me, at the time I wasn't aware that a Duncan McTavish existed."

Mr. McTavish looked even more puzzled. "I don't understand..." he began.

Marilla took a deep breath. She struggled to find the right words to help this stranger comprehend why she would ever do such a thing. She hoped she also would begin to understand herself.

"You see, in a small place like Avonlea, it is very difficult to have anything of your own...any experience...any memory. Everyone knows all about everyone else...and therefore everyone knows that Marilla Cuthbert has never been the object...of anyone's affections."

Marilla's voice trembled, and Mr. McTavish looked down at his shoes, suddenly uncomfortable.

"Please, you don't have to tell me this..."

"Yes," insisted Marilla. "I want you to understand. I have no idea what possessed me...pride, I suppose. But I did make you up. I created a beau for the benefit of the ladies of the sewing circle. My favorite name has always been Duncan, and what should my eyes light upon but an advertisement for McTavish's Porous Plasters. And so you were born, Duncan McTavish, from New Brunswick, but feared to be out West. It wasn't right of me to tell such a tale. But who would have ever supposed there was a real Duncan McTavish? I have never heard of such a coincidence."

Marilla looked Mr. McTavish straight in the eye, pleading with him silently. She did not want or deserve to be vindicated from all blame, but it was vitally important to her that he understand her motives. She turned her gaze across the lawn, trying to maintain some dignity in the face of such an undignified situation. There really wasn't any more to be said. She felt as if a great weight had been lifted from her shoulders.

Mr. McTavish shook his head in disbelief. Suddenly, he started to chuckle, and his chuckle grew until it was full-fledged laughter.

Marilla looked up at him in surprise, thinking at first that the man must be mad, but his laughter was infectious, and soon the very hint of a smile appeared at the edges of her mouth. Marilla could see that Mr. McTavish was in fact genuinely amused at the whole situation, and in her relief, she began to laugh as well. Their combined laughter filled the garden, and the more they laughed the more contagious it became. Duncan McTavish put his hand on Marilla's shoulder to steady himself as mirth overtook both of them.

The sound of their hilarity reached the ears of an astonished Rachel Lynde and a very relieved and pleased Sara Stanley. As Rachel observed these two people talking and chuckling together, she was suddenly struck with the horror of realization. She had doubted Marilla, her best friend on this earth, when obviously everything Marilla had said about Duncan McTavish was quite true. They did know each other. It was obvious. Didn't the gentleman just put his arm on Marilla's shoulder as if it were the most natural thing in the world for him to do? No stranger would be that forward. Rachel's mouth fell open with the enormity of her insight. She stood there, a picture of penitence.

Sara looked sideways at Mrs. Lynde and realized exactly what was going through her mind. She, on the other hand, felt no such pangs of guilt. She beamed with self-satisfaction in the knowledge that, despite how black things had seemed, a little bit of human intervention hadn't hurt in the end.

Outside, Mr. McTavish and Marilla had gained some control of themselves and were now laughing quite comfortably and enjoying each other's company. They walked slowly across the lawn towards the gate.

"Well, I'm not a Methodist, so our way is

clear!" said Mr. McTavish with a twinkle in his eye. "It's time we made up that old quarrel, don't you think?"

Marilla found herself blushing like a schoolgirl, quite cheerful in her relief. "Well, Mr. McTavish, I appreciate your understanding."

As they reached the white picket gate, Mr. McTavish turned to Marilla with a mischievous smile on his handsome face. "In fact, I have just thought of a wonderful way to still the tongues of all those sewing circle buzzards! Are you interested?"

Marilla looked quizzical.

Straining her neck to see what they were up to, Rachel could just make out that the pair were still conversing and laughing at the gate. "What on earth are they doing?" questioned Rachel. "Are they going to plant themselves by that gate until the cows come home?"

Marilla smiled and shook her head in indecision.

"Well, Mr. McTavish, I'm old-fashioned enough to believe that two wrongs do not make a right." Her mouth twisted into a smile in spite of herself. "Nevertheless, I don't see what harm it could do."

"I'm glad you agree," replied Mr. McTavish heartily. He smiled and tipped his hat to her. "Until Sunday, then."

"Good day, Mr. McTavish," said Marilla as she

opened the gate. Mr. McTavish bowed in a courtly manner and left. Marilla waved goodbye as the gentleman climbed into his buggy and, waving back, drove away, whistling to himself.

For a moment, Marilla felt just like a girl of eighteen again. The color rose in her cheeks, her eyes shone, and if anyone had been watching, they would have said that, at that moment, the years literally fell away from Marilla Cuthbert.

Sensible woman that she was, however, Marilla straightened her shoulders and, looking towards the curtained windows of the sitting room as they gave a telltale twitch, she headed towards the house to face the last bit of business with which she had to deal.

Chapter Twenty

Rachel snapped the sitting room curtains shut and walked in a near daze towards the door to the hall. Sara followed in her wake, barely concealing her relief and joy at the way things had turned out.

Marilla entered the front hall of Green Gables, closing the door softly behind her. She looked around, fully expecting to come face to face with an accusing Rachel, but seeing no one, she headed thoughtfully towards the stairs.

There was the unmistakable creak of the sitting room door opening, and Marilla stopped halfway up the stairs and looked down at a stricken Rachel, with Sara behind her.

Rachel wrung her hands in despair. "How can you forgive me, Marilla?" she asked, in a voice that quavered. "I doubted your word, I admit it. I thought that I knew everything about you there was to know, but I was wrong." She looked down at the carpet remorsefully. "I'm not one who can never be brought to own up that they've made a mistake."

Marilla looked uncomfortable and took a deep breath. What must be done, must be done.

"Really, Rachel, there is no need..." she began, but as usual, Rachel Lynde was not about to listen to anyone else but herself.

"You should throw me out of this house this very minute!" she said dramatically. "Mr. McTavish was your beau, I realize that now."

Marilla looked ceilingward. "He was nothing of the sort, Rachel. I met him for the first time this very day."

Her statement was met with a momentary silence of disbelief. Sara bit her lip, her eyes as round as saucers. Rachel could do nothing but stare, and her mouth dropped as yet another wave of emotions washed over her in her confusion.

Marilla fastened a look on the astonished
Sara. "And Sara, now you understand why you
must never lie. Because you will always regret
it." She looked at Rachel, her steely blue eyes
softening at the realization of what she had put
her companion through. "Rachel, my dear, good
friend. It is I who should be begging your for-
giveness. I am truly sorry."

Poor Rachel stood motionless, still not quite
able to grasp the reality of the situation, as
Marilla continued slowly up the stairs. Sara was
equally taken aback. She was trying to figure out
where human intervention had ended and
Providence had taken over. It slowly began to
dawn on her that, in view of what she had just
witnessed, human intervention aside, Providence
certainly seemed to be on Marilla and Mr.
McTavish's side.

Chapter Twenty-one

The bells rang out joyfully and the good and
devout people of Avonlea filed out of the pretty
white clapboard church the following Sunday
morning. Reverend Leonard shook hands with
his flock as they strolled out into the bright sunshine.

The grown-ups socialized while the children raced about in the pure relief of being outside, no longer expected to sit silent and straight in the hard pews of the church.

Janet King could be seen deep in conversation with Olivia and Hetty. Alec caught up on the latest village news with Mr. Lawson. Cecily giggled with her friend Clemmie Rae and Felicity primped, hoping that someone would notice her new hat with the real silk violets on it. Andrew and Felix punched each other in the arms for no apparent reason until Janet threw a baleful look at them and put a stop to it.

Rachel Lynde surveyed the crowd. She was resplendent in a large, beige hat with feathers that must have made life very difficult for the poor soul who had happened to sit in the pew directly behind her. Sara emerged from the church, wearing a dress of soft, pastel hues, cinched at the waist and complemented by a matching ribbon in her hat. She made her way towards Mrs. Lynde to say hello.

Mrs. Potts bustled out of the church, obviously with a bee in her bonnet. Reverend Leonard offered her his hand and she hurriedly said her salutations and thanks, but her eyes scanned the crowd. Then, spotting exactly who she was looking for, she lost no time in sidling over to Rachel.

Good, she thought to herself. That Sara Stanley is with her, too. Two birds with one stone, she chuckled. She tapped Rachel smartly on the shoulder. "Rachel Lynde?"

Rachel looked down at Mrs. Potts very coolly indeed, observing her with no trace of Christian charity in her eyes whatsoever.

Mrs. Potts was not to be put off by Rachel's demeanor. "I suppose you heard of my meeting with Duncan McTavish. And it wasn't about Porous Plasters, either," she said coyly.

Rachel Lynde was not amused. "I heard about it, Mrs. Potts," she said shortly.

Sara, overhearing this exchange, looked with dread at Mrs. Lynde, praying as she hadn't even prayed in church that she would not betray any of her privileged knowledge.

Mrs. Potts looked smug. "I never gave credence to Marilla Cuthbert's story and I never will!"

Rachel drew herself up to her full height and breadth and, to Sara's delight, proceeded to give Mrs. Potts a long overdue piece of her mind.

"Mrs. Potts, it's gossips like you that give women a bad name. Why don't you open your eyes and close your mouth."

With that, Rachel gave a pointed look towards the road. Sara drew in her breath in delight. A buggy had appeared and was approaching them at a clip, Mr. Duncan McTavish holding the reins. As he drew up in front of the church, the whole congregation watched and waited in anticipation of what might happen.

Heads turned as one as Marilla Cuthbert appeared on the steps of the church and shook hands with Reverend Leonard. Sara smiled to herself. Marilla looked beautiful. She was wearing a printed blouse of cornflower blue, the very match of her eyes. Her hat was new and flattered her immensely. She watched with everyone else as Marilla looked around and spotted Mr. McTavish. She smiled graciously at him, and slowly walked through the gaping crowd towards the buggy.

"Allow me, Miss Cuthbert," said a dashing Mr. Duncan McTavish. He leapt out of the buggy and came around to her side to assist her gallantly to her seat. The crowd began to buzz.

"Thank you, Mr. McTavish," said Marilla, in her low voice, as clear as a bell.

"A fine day, isn't it?" remarked Mr. McTavish as he took his place beside her.

"One to remember," she said, as she flashed him a brilliant smile.

They gave each other a small wink and at a flick of the reins, the buggy pulled away. Sara grinned and waved, catching Marilla's eye.

Marilla smiled back at her and, with a tiny,

barely perceptible wink, waved her handkerchief as the buggy traveled away down the road.

Next to Sara, Rachel waved heartily and then turned with a smile to Mrs. Potts, who stood rooted to the spot beside her. Then Mrs. Potts gave a "Hmmph!" and walked away in a huff.

Sara looked up at Rachel with new respect and undisguised appreciation. She realized that, underneath it all, Mrs. Lynde was indeed Marilla Cuthbert's true friend and would never in her life willingly betray her. Rachel looked down at the grinning Sara, and they exchanged the look of true conspirators.

"You're never too old to tell a little white lie, Sara," said Mrs. Lynde, "or keep a secret, that's what!"

Sara smiled and nodded in understanding.

Mrs. Lawson and her niece sighed and waved as Marilla drove away.

"There! You see? I knew it all along. Marilla Cuthbert is the soul of honesty," said Mrs. Lawson, well pleased at how events had unfolded.

Her niece appeared as if she would swoon at any moment. "Oh, and it's so romantic, I could just die!" she exclaimed.

Felicity came up to Sara with Cecily. "What was all that about?" she asked, wondering what Sara was looking so happy and smug about.

"Oh nothing," said Sara. "Just that it's so nice that Duncan McTavish and Marilla Cuthbert got together. See?" She pointed to the buggy disappearing in the distance. "Isn't it wonderful?"

Felix and Andrew joined the girls at that moment, but overhearing the tone of the conversation, rolled their eyes in mock disgust.

"Let's get out of here, Andrew," said Felix. "I'd rather go back into church than listen to this mush." The boys sauntered off in the other direction.

Sara was too happy to let them bother her, and Felicity wondered at her unshakable good mood.

"I don't know why you look so smug, Sara Stanley. It's not as if you were responsible. They were bound to get together, no matter what."

Sara raised an eyebrow. "Maybe. Maybe not."

"I heard that they had a secret meeting and Mr. McTavish proposed," said Cecily, her eyes shining at the very thought.

Not to be outdone, Felicity added her two cents' worth to the conversation. "Well, people say that Marilla turned him down because her love for Green Gables was stronger."

"Sara, isn't that just the most romantic thing you ever heard?" asked Cecily.

In the distance, Sara could just make out Marilla Cuthbert and Duncan McTavish, as the buggy swept along the red gravel road towards the sea.

Sara looked at her cousins with a knowing smile. "Don't believe anything you hear, girls, and only half of what you see!"

❧   ❧   ❧